Incredibly Selfish

by

Duncan Lyon

Published by Palm House Publishing
Copyright © 2016 Duncan Lyon
All rights reserved.

ISBN-13: 978-0-9934466-1-0

DEDICATION

Edward Rushton (1756-1814)

The drizzle on the cobbles in the early morning

That's my Liverpool

Half-eaten butty and your laces undone

You're going to be late for school!

A ship with a cargo of containers coming in through the locks

A bus with a cartload of hangovers going down to the docks

My Liverpool's a city of dogs and kids all kicking up in the street

Won't you give that dog a bone Ma?

Give that kid a sweet

And the people know how to treat a stranger

See that open door

If you've never had a plate of my Ma's scouse then you've never lived before.

Theme from "Jakestown" (from memory)

Written and sung by Brian Jacques

"Hörst du den nicht dieses furchtbare Geschrei um dich herum? Das Gaschrei, das man Schweigen nennt!"

Don't you hear that horrible screaming all around you? The screaming that men call silence!

from "The Enigma of Kaspar Hauser" by Werner Herzog

"Riesci a sentire la voce della molle?   I Romani la chiamorono 'acque felici'."

Can you hear the voice of the springs?   The Romans called it 'happy waters'.

From "8 ½" by Federico Fellini

Someone could do with a bowl of noodles. Someone somewhere could murder a Rustler's burger.

I should explain in case the experts can't:

A man who has been assigned the name "McKelnikov" was approaching the corner of St Anne Street & Islington when he first received a text. It was from Joanne and she was telling him what had happened with Elvis or to be clearer she was telling him what had happened with Elvis's mum. He put his phone away and carried on towards London Road. It was a bright and sunny Sunday morning and there was nobody else around. Meanwhile, a few hundred yards behind him, this happened –

"This should have been done earlier. If you do it at the same time it's a much easier job."

"I feel awful, Paul. I was rushed. I didn't hardly have a chance."

"You have to try, Pauline. I know it isn't easy but it's the only way to make sense of it. As you're talking and taking the call you make two sets of notes. One for you and one for dispatch. You've got nothing."

"I know. I got into a panic. He wouldn't stop. It was the first time I've had anything like that."

"Can you remember anything he said?"

"Not really. There was too much of a noise."

"Let me listen to the recording and see if we can make anything out."

"I'm sorry, Paul. This is harder than I thought."

"You'll get used to it."

"I hope so. My nerves are gone already."

"Go on, you'll be alright. Take it from the top. Let's have a crack together."

A flicker of paper is cast into the breeze. We see McKelnikov as he passes deserted side-streets. He is thinking of nights-out that became mornings-after, back when he and Elvis had been running around town, when they were still the best of mates and as close as some brothers. 'Go anywhere twice, second time to apologise'. Fascinations in girls and music and football, football and music and girls, everything sub-subjected within architecture, morality, politics, revolution... all in each day with hourly updates. The city is still the same but the world has shrunk towards it. Where he turns on to Lime Street there is a hidden sense of silent whispers where the first settlements stood; a mildly idyllic-seeming fishing village, almost out of ordinary sight but

12

interrupted and imposed upon by monks trading their ways and their thinking, interference from over water, a population swollen by doubling generations. He imagines himself watching the city grow, hearing its songs and growls and howls as it stretches and reaches out, the clanking shove of slavery chains, privateering blasts and the weary fall of immigrants spilling ashore.

He guessed that she had become unwell over time. He thought of how long it had taken his own mother to pass. The two women, from their own angles, had seen the best of the city when it had been all the rage. Elvis's mum was a teacher from one of the finer suburbs. His was a nurse. Both in their ways seemed innocent and certain, formidable and fearful. Liverpool girls, who looked upon the other's son with recognition, a familiarity that here is the one who will fight with their fights, see the other through every heartbreak, pull them out of any riot, that they'd conquer whatever was waiting. But there hadn't really been any riots to speak of and now the sound of shutters brought him back into the moment.

*

"Are you getting anything?"

"Bits."

"Do you want me to rewind it?"

"I don't know. There was something. There's not much we can do about the background.   There's the...is it the..?"

"What?"

"I don't know. Wind. Water. Wind."

"It isn't easy is it?"

"You're right, like, with all the noise..."

"Is it English?"

"I... I'm betting yes. Go on. Go back again. I'm going to need a coffee. We'll listen... In a minute. Give me two minutes. I'll be back in a couple of minutes."

*

He thinks again about the message.

Jo had said politely, diplomatically, that she didn't know if he'd heard the news. He counts off the stone lions across the plateau, looking for a separate expression in each of their faces. They hadn't heard from or spoken to each other properly in years. He'd decided long ago that the reason for this was that he'd allowed himself to drift so deeply into his work that he'd taken on a peculiarity of personality. He had let himself be taken over. A couple of accidental encounters aside - outside a train station, Elvis sat in his car waiting, or on the edge of a crowd when the head-the-balls came to try to walk through the town – the meetings were few. That was the last time. Last summer. He was there with his little girl who would have been about five by then, she'd been skipping around amongst all the red and yellow flags being waved about down by the Pier Head. She hadn't known what was going on and didn't know who McKelnikov was, although they'd half put on a little pretense as if she did, just for the sake of it, to make it feel a little bit less awkward. She was naturally shy and Old Elvo had never been any good with awkward. That was one of the ways in which they'd always been different. Elvis works for the council, in one of their offices. He does this, almost invisibly.

In the unlit units on Cazneau Street he sees little of his personal reflection, only the morning night-collar taxis as they achingly roll to rest. Yet still he is able to convince himself that he is crucial to the well-being of the circus. He goes wherever he thinks is necessary; backwards, forwards, sideways, he stops and starts again. It is a life of some sort of sacrifice. It hadn't been decided upon. It had just happened. He imagines and accepts that he'd been on some sort of list, drawn into a role created especially. He stops beneath the glass canopy at the entrance to Central Station. A street-sweeper churns by. He checks to see if anyone is at the ticket barriers inside. The screen, the neon scroll: New Brighton, Chester, West Kirkby, Southport, Hunts Cross, New Brighton, Chester, West Kirkby, Southport, Hunts Cross. On one of the pillars next to where he stands is something marked into thick corporate yellow paint: scraped with a key or a pen-knife in quick vertical triangular letters. He touches at it with his finger. A small flake of paint picks off and he catches it in his palm. He wonders at the time it would have taken to scratch it out and who might have been bored and distracted enough to do it. In this day and age. With cameras everywhere. All Ordinary, it says.

"80s.", he thinks. "Dead dead 80s."

The screens go blank for a few seconds and then the same words reappear: Chester, West Kirkby, Southport, Hunts Cross, New Brighton, Chester, West Kirkby, Southport, Hunts Cross, New Brighton.

He thinks of what he should text to Joanne. He sends a message to say 'thanks for letting me know' and heads to the Tabac for a think.

*

"Nothing in this world surprises me.", announces Tilly as she shifts from one cheek to the other. "I've seen it all before, as you know."

"Lift your feet up there, queen."

"I'd like to see how these ones would thingy."

"No excuse." mutters Maria as she revs up the Ewbank and attacks the rug in front of the chair.

"They've got it easier than Soft Joe. If you want hard luck stories you can have them: Mrs Aquiano's father-in-law, Mr Levi, he was up there in the heights of the May Blitz, gone right off his cake on the top of the tenements, his hair all white and stood up on end and there's him, waving about his home-made schnapps at the Luftwaffe, shouting all the Ukrainian odds he was, while the bombs were falling all the way along. They planted one right smack bong – bang! - at the top end of Greek Street and his bottle exploded in his hands. He was lit up head to toe in the overcoat she's got him from Blacklers."

She lights another menthol while Maria empties the ashtray.

"And they got hit and all."

"Who did?"

"Blacklers! You listening or am I talking to the ghost? Our Michael helped bring him down, which he shouldn't have done."

"Oh don't, Nan."

"Everyone crying their eyes out. They were no more than bits of kids. Ten, twelve, eleven. But they said they couldn't leave him. God love them. The seagulls, rats..."

"Do you want these papers?"

"You just get on with it don't you?"

"I'll put them in one pile."

Tilly looks around for her handbag.

"Is your mam coming over today?"

"She says she might do. She might not. She's up the wall."

"What is it now?"

"Only the usual."

"Help me up, love."

"Your bath's not ready yet. Finish your ciggy. Where's

your purse?"

"I seen him, you know."

"You said."

"He didn't see me. I called over to him but he was walking along. He was with Prince."

"I hate them, I hate the pair of them."

"Ah he loves that Prince."

"I'm very happy for them."

"Well he hasn't got anything else. It gets him out."

"Yeah, looking half dug-up. I'd be... I'm just fed up of him."

"Oh Maria..."

"I don't like talking about him, Nan. He's a waste of my time. Doesn't come round here does he? Doesn't come in to see how you are."

"I shouldn't have said anything. I only get shouted at."

"Do you want these papers or what? Do I launch them?"

"I'll look at them later. I save the crosswords for when no-one comes."

"You want to cut them out. Less mess. They attract mice. And listen to you, hard lines Annie, you'd think you're forever on your own. That's my thanks? Like I haven't got my own running around to do."

"Ah give over, I haven't got mice."

"Be company for you though. Eh? Sure our Kevin would be pleased. He's here yesterday with the girls. Eddie brought your tea in last night. And here's you, the lonely old woman who lived in a whatsname. And here's me, harassed, like the Olympic flame compared to you, me, I am."

"You're picking on me now."

"Where were when you seen him?"

"Going for me messages. Going about my business."

"On the way to the alehouse, you mean. Bet you tell them, all your cronies, bet you tell all them we've abandoned you as well."

"I only pop in for the news, for a bit of a jangle."

"Gallivanting. That's what it is. You going for a little toddle this avvy?"

"I might do. What's it looking like?"

"Nice. It was lovely first thing. Looks like you'll have a

nice day."

"Oh good. I like a nice day."

"See how you are after a bit of brekky eh?"

"Don't do me too much, girl. Or do what you want and you have what I can't manage."

"Up you get then, Lady May. Your stick's here when you want it."

"Come on then. Jesus tonight. Oo-er, Maria, look at me. I'm like the arse end of a pantomime horse."

"Here you go. Take your time. Nice and slow. Straighten up. That's better."

"Just do me half a plate, love. I'm not like you. I go off it if there's too much to look at. Don't rush me. Let my leg warm up a bit. That's it. There's some smoked Irish out there our Eddie brought in, from off one of his mates. Do us a couple of pieces and take the rest for the kids. I won't eat a whole packet. But don't say anything. Oof! Lord Jesus. He doesn't mean any harm."

*

If he was to catch anyone's attention it might be said that he has the mechanical movement that comes with some light military training – an evenness of weight, precise – but with a restraint, a relaxation that bleeds into resignation. The effect makes him fade and almost dissolve from sight. There is nobody inside the café as he enters. His brow is cloaked in a scarlet darkness as his eyes adjust to the light. Years ago when a hippy called Ped had it everything was the other way around. He remembers it as being seething with goodwill. The tables were so close together that the mismatched chairs clattered into one another with each weave in and climb out. He looks around at the screwed down silver tables and blood-red cushioned benches, all devilishly ordered and neat. He reads from the list of breakfasts and burgers, white-painted like chalk on a broad blackboard. The waitress appears directly in front of him behind the counter. He hadn't seen her. She looks Spanish, he thinks. Portuguese. No, Spanish. Dark hair, perhaps jet black in this low light, held up in a high wavy ponytail with dramatic liner and lashes, deeply distant high sharp cheekbones and strong straight nose, different, somehow regal. He projects a movie through his mind; through generations of wickedly cautious Counts and voraciously sensual swirling Contessas, castle-bound, in sky-high spiraling turrets. And here she comes, this one, here, escaped, to this place, this city, at this time...

and…

"Yes? Hello? You like to order?"

He asks for a coffee. She points up at a list. He says the first one he sees. She asks if she can get him anything else and he asks for an orange juice. He looks around and nods towards a seat in the corner. He goes and sits within a sharpening triangle of sunlight.

He hasn't got Elvis's number so he goes through Messenger. He types and deletes, types and deletes, types and deletes. At the end he reads:

"Had a message from Jo. Sorry to hear your sad news. God bless."

*

She is completing her first standard post of the morning. It is entitled "15 things to do today in Liverpool". She has copied and pasted nine of the 'things' from across previous weeks, changed a few of the photos and managed a paragraph or two for some new ones. She runs a spell-check through everything and reads through quickly once more, then transfers the document into a publication file. She reviews the formatting. She clicks on all of the social media icons

23

and presses GO. She refreshes the Twitter and Facebook feeds to check that it has appeared and looks as it should. She reaches into her bag and takes out her phone and looks again on her own pages. Everything seems correct. She has eighteen minutes before she has to prepare another. She slightly opens the lid on her coffee to see if it is still worth drinking. She takes a sip and closes it back over, sits back in her chair, pushes back from the desk and thinks about what it might be like to be somewhere else, right now, somewhere else, at this moment. Somewhere different. Somewhere she is free, can feel adventurous. Somewhere with 150 things to do, that can't all be written down.

She closes her eyes and imagines. She goes.

*

"He's saying, right, he's said 'What do you do if you see a man on a roof? What do you do if he isn't doing anything? If he's just there, sat there or standing there and you are only one who sees him? What do you actually do?' And that's about it. There's more but I think it might be just more of the same, I think."

"Frigging hell, Pauline. How've you done that?"

"It took a while."

"Superb."

"Ta."

"No, I mean it."

"I just, you know, I just had a go."

"You've done great though. You really have. Ten out of ten. Top marks. Good on you."

"Oh well."

"I'll make a note of all this. I mean it. I'm impressed."

"You just do your best don't you?"

"You certainly do."

"What do I do with it now?"

"I don't know really, to be honest. But well done. That was really, really good."

*

It doesn't feel right but he sends it anyway. It doesn't read well at all. He has time to think and send something else if it comes to him. He guesses that Elvis will be sleeping for a while. He can see that he was last active five hours ago so assumes that he will have been drinking til late. That's usually what happens.

The waitress brings over the coffee. He nods and muffles a 'thanks' then reproaches himself for not saying it in Spanish. When she goes out of sight he feels uncomfortably left on his own. He is gladdened when a sharp sound brings relief, a repetitive guitar riff barking through the speakers. Passenger, loud. The volume comes down as the drums roll in. When the waitress returns it feels more intimate, less claustrophobic. There seems to be a softer light with the sounds on. He sees she is quietly singing shahadah-like with the chorus.

"a la-la la-la, la-la-la laaa..."

He watches an empty 82 yawn its way out of town. His gaze settles on elbowing figures at the bottom of the steps to the Bombed Out Church, gathering up odds between them. A gentle mist of Chinese students drift by. The clunk of a glass on his table makes his head turn as the waitress is stepping outside into the sunshine. She lightens several shades, leans weightlessly against a lamppost and carefully sparks a roll-up.

She turns and looks at him through the full length windows. He feels as if he looks as if he is talking to himself. She carries on staring until he feels he has to go out to her.

*

"Get out of bed kidda. Come 'ed. Before she kicks off."

"I will in a minute."

"We've forgotten what you look like. Come on."

"Leave off."

"Come on!"

"I will in a minute!"

"You're awake now."

"So?"

"So… You know… Rise and shine and that. Shake a leg. Get a shift on. All that gear. All that stuff. Morning has broken. Aren't you going to do anything useful today? I said…"

"I heard."

"Well then?"

"Well then what?"

"When I was your age…"

"Aaagh!"

"What was that, our little ray of sunshine?"

"You heard. I said 'Aaagh'."

"Turn round, I can't hear you.   Why did you say 'Aaagh'?"

"'My age'."

"Yeah.   'Your age'. We'd be out and about, making a crust, chasing bits of birds around."

"My age though."

"What, like? What about it?"

"You was never my age."

"Ha! Come on though. Up you get. Don't be a shitbag all your life."

"This is my age."

"Oh aye?"

"Yeah. This is my age. You had your age. This is my age."

"I see, yeah."

"Yeah. See."

"Yeah. Well. Yeah. You've got me there. I tell you what. Why don't you go back to college? What do you say to that? Go to uni? Fill in one of their forms?"

"Yeah alright."

"I'm serious. Why don't you?"

"What for?"

"Go on a course."

"To do what?"

"Fucking philosophy you smartarsed little cunt. 'Your age'. Now get up before she's back and I get it in the neck. And open the fucking windows. It stinks in here. I've fucking told you! Now look lively for fuck's sake or I'll have to properly properly batter you. I'll do you a three handed lift and I'll fart on your head. Now come on."

"You're not even funny."

"And you can go the shop. There's no hot water."

"This is shit."

"What?"

"Nothing."

"Don't make me angry. You won't like me when I'm angry."

"I don't like you now."

"Shift! Dickhead."

*

She takes a pouch of tobacco out of her back pocket and is about to hand it to him when he gets a buzz on his phone. He doesn't want to answer but when he sees the notification message he opens the map. There's a glowering red blob in the middle. It is in the middle of Upper Frederick Street, well within walking distance. She has been watching and is still looking now. He shrugs a little, finishes the glass, takes the five pound note out of his pocket, leans inside and drops it on the table.

"I just...gracias, anyway."

Everything sticks and stops as he turns.

Almost everything changes.

His vision sweeps...bleeding horizontally, stretching,

oscillating, rainbow…ever so slowly.

There's an impact in his mind, within his sight - a brightness that briefly effervesces, a surrounding magnesium flash of colour and light. No sound, no sound save for…

…the streeeeeeetching of slooooowness…

For these moments, there is only the sun. There is nothing else.

And then, in one more, in another step, it all comes back – the street, the lamp-posts, the shops, the cafes, the world - from within an almighty vanishing point. Only an afterglow remains.

Beat. Beat. Beat.

Changing. Chaining. Change.

*

"Look at the state of your trousers!"

"It's mud, mostly, I think."

"Where's your effin boots?"

"In the van."

"Oh sound. Nice one. Why's that then?"

"He was down on the banks, wasn't he? The whopper."

"What banks?"

"Mudbanks."

"Ok. What do you mean by mudbanks?"

"Like sandbanks but they're not. It's all mud. You know, the river? The tide was out. He was running round on the bloody whatdoyoucallit, on the shore, on the riverbed. It's all mud. Down by the Pier Head and along near the Echo. He's gone over the railings, down the friggin steps, onto all this sludge, this mud, slipping and sliding, banging a tambourine, carrying on shocking. You'd think he was in bleeding Ibiza."

"Where's the tambourine?"

"In the van."

"Brilliant."

"Yeah, so..."

"You're not bringing him in here if he's anything like your keks."

"What will I do with him?"

"I've got half an hour, no tell a lie, eighteen minutes before I go off duty. I'm not getting a mop and bucket out now."

"What are we supposed to do?"

"You are covered in...shite."

"Black lad, you see. Black male."

"So?"

"Black as the ace of spades now, like. Thinks it's funny. It wasn't though. It was grim."

"Come on. Out. Come on. I mean it. This is no good. Away, come on. Outside."

"There he is. Grinning, look. And he's worse than us."

"So, what's his game? What do we know?"

"Crank job isn't he? We had to go and get him. He could have got stuck. The tide and that. I don't know."

"Not the full shilling then?"

"Well he was laughing his head off when we were chasing him. Singing his head off as well. He wrote something in the sand with a stick."

"Oh yeah?"

"Yeah."

"Well? Go on?"

"It said 'Under the paving stones the bleach'."

"Smashing. You said mud before."

"Dave isn't happy either, near fell flat on his face in front of everyone."

"I'll see to this in the meantime but in the meantime you stink."

"I know. I'm knocking myself sick."

"Hundreds of years' worth of shabite you're caked in. Let me have a think. Go and wait over there. Well away, go on, all of you, away from the doors. Go on, over there in the far corner. And stop him from laughing. I don't know, tell him your life story. I don't really care, lad. Give him a big kiss. Use your initiative."

*

"Hiya love."

"Oh hello girl. You alright?"

"I'm fine, babe. Everyone there ok?"

"Getting along, you know. What's to do?"

"I know you're going into work soon…"

"I'm on the bus now."

"Go on then. I just wanted to ask you if you've got that number, is all."

"Ah, you won't regret it, Cath. She's properly amazing."

"I'll give it a go. What have you got to lose?"

"You won't believe it."

"If you say so, that she's good…"

"Oh she is."

"You never know."

"Oh I know. But believe me, you'll be…oh you just have to see for yourself. She's…oh she's just…"

"So what do you actually do? What does she do?"

"You don't do anything. You just go."

"Does she use…what does she use?"

"She doesn't use anything. She can use something if you want, but she doesn't have to use anything."

"So I don't need to take anything?"

"Just yourself."

"That's all I've got."

"But Cathy, listen, if I tell you: so I've walked in haven't I and she's said to me, no word of a lie, just looked at me in the hallway and she turns round and goes 'wait, wait, don't tell me anything, don't tell me a thing, nothing about yourself, let me feel the...you know...', and then she tells me straight, everything about what had happened, all with our Louie and the Valentes and how there was the thing, and all the leg and how long it was for and how I was always thinking about my grand-dad and how much I miss him."

"Oh I know love."

"And all about our Steven and everything."

"Oh eh Deanne. She sound's marvellous."

"She's got the gift. What can you say?"

"Where does she do it?"

"In her house. In Tuebrook. You get off by the Coconut Grove. I'll text you the number. I'm just getting to my stop now, love. Give me a minute and I'll..."

"And how much does she..?"

"Thirty five pounds."

"Cash alright?"

"I think she prefers that, yeah."

"Alright love. Thanks love. I'll let you go then."

"I've told her you might call. Give her a bell in an hour or two. I'll have to go or he will race right past my stop."

"I know hun, they're lunatics. T-ra love. Go on then. I'll let you go. Take care. Say... You still there, love? Hello! No. You've gone."

*

He distracts himself with many of the same different windows. His pace quickens as his senses settle and he calculates the quickest way to go.

The store-fronts feel oppressive: bets on football, bets on horses, bets on package holidays, late holidays, trainers, shirts, shoes, handbags, phones, dresses, sunglasses, computers, holidays, trainers, dresses, jackets, washing machines, televisions.

Windows grow larger as he goes.   Huge clean

reflectionless windows.   Circular sightlines of black bowled cameras at every corner. He steers and veers to the shadows but they don't quite reach the ground.

All the walking through.

Pretending, pretending to look, watching, reading or trying to read, comparing expressions, imagining, witnessing, bearing witness, staying close while staying away, guessing from other people's intentions.

He has to get on otherwise he has no purpose.

Bear left towards Upper Frederick Street.

Beat.

*

He wakes up alone.

He wakes up alone again.

These days he wakes up alone.

These days, these days there is only a small stolen space in which to remain peaceful. It won't be more than a moment until he has become himself, his newer more recent self; become angry, like the anger is there in the room and it has grown impatient waiting, just for him, staring at him, waiting til he opens his eyes. It demands to be made welcome and almost immediately he is made aware. He becomes conscious of being awake but it comes to him these days, these days within a perceptible sense of dread. Something wants to pounce. He will remember something soon. He will know what is down for him, what the day has ready, in a long short second. It could be any of one of a dozen reminding words or pictures. What strength he still has within him is in trying to create something out of the narrowness in which he feels trapped. By the time he has turned on the hot water tap he'll already have found himself forced to vent his frustrations at one or another inanimate object – a door, a discarded shoe, another door - that has refused to co-operate or gotten in his way, already!!!, again!!!, and he is close to despairing, already!!!, again!!!

He finds it hard to consider calmly but his routine is all he has to help him to settle a few of his rawest nerves. What day is it anyway? But what does it bastard well matter. If he thinks of himself as if he is already absent perhaps there is something that can be made out of it. If he tells himself he is dead already it is only to see if it makes him feel any better.

A word. A word is enough. Half a word that proves he is alive, not dead.

Yesterday the word had been...

Tomorrow it would be...

The moment of realisation. His world rushes in on itself.

He feels hateful for quite a bit of the next few minutes. Full of a hate. He has nowhere to go to escape from it, nobody to see and no reason to be without it. The day is a blank page to him and he feels enforced to make a mess of everything. He only ever makes things worse. It's just how he is, these days. The only way to avoid it all if he stays in his bed but he can't be doing that again. He thinks he probably did that all day yesterday.

The sunshine glows through his curtains forcing a darkly bright crimson. He half-opens the narrowest of them. He kicks over a cushion across the floor to prop the door open. He goes into the bathroom and turns off the tap. He changes the station on the radio and increases the volume to where he can just about hear it without listening. He goes into the kitchen, fills the kettle and forgets to switch it on.

He subdues, softens and smothers the anger as the worst of it peaks but all the same he is sick of it – he detests it – he hates it all the same.

*

On Paradise Street now.

A couple of security guards are starting their shifts, they loosen and straighten their ties. McKelnikov dances and dodges the hoses that splash the walkways in front of the stores. His vision swerves unsteadily. He escapes from the hulk of Liverpool One into and through the narrow brown brick alleyways, to the open space of the last lost estate in town; done up in faded dun pebbledash with closed over upstairs curtains, mobility cars edged up onto pavements, lace and lightly tended gardens. He can picture the day that the bulldozers will come and rage it all into a cinder-strewn car park. There are no cameras here. He can see along the street a crowd scene crouched around a police car. Older residents are gathered and as he gets closer he hears their what-abouts and I-don't-knows. One of the uniforms is taking charge and trying to cajole them away from the pavement.

"Jesus tonight, he's causing murder."

"This is all of that stuff."

He sees who is creating. It is a young man stood on the roof of a bungalow, standing high up on the top of a chimney-stack. He presents a pale, blank staring expression. He is straight and still against a clear blue hollow sky. He is wearing a black t-shirt and grey jogging pants, and gives a strange impression as if...as if he's some sort of a vertical human aerial. He is reading from his phone with one hand raised to shield the screen from the sun. He wobbles a little for a moment like a high wire walker, then steadies again. But it is the expression. The palest grey blanking expression.

"Bebebeen up there fufuf...", mutters an old man.

"For an hour.", finishes one of the women.

"Susususus..."

"Someone will have to go up to him."

The constables look silently to one another.

"It's only a baybobabungalow. Our bebaby c-could jump that."

There are more tuts from the women.

"What's he doing now, Jean?"

"Oh he's having a gr-gr-great time."

"Ah leave him alone, he's only a baby himself."

"Has he had anything to eat?"

Jean shouts up to him: "Have you had anything to eat,

42

Jordan love?"

He looks down only for a moment. He frowns faintly and goes back to his phone.

"Do him a sandwich and he can have it when he wants it."

"Shall I do you a burger, love? They only take a minute."

"Do him some noodles, Jean."

"Do you want some of your noodles?"

One of the women mouths carefully to him: "Are you alright, love?"

"S-s-s-s-s-s-starve him down."

"Go home, Joe!"

"Horror."

"Take him home, Elaine. He's getting on my wick."

McKelnikov backs away and leaves them to it. He doesn't know anyone. No-one has taken any notice of him approaching. He leaves the way he came.

*

"You must let go of your hat. I can't do anything with you until you let go of your hat."

"It said 'beach', not bleach. What would bleach mean?"

"I don't know. Are you going to give me the hat?"

"It doesn't even make sense."

"Oh. It doesn't make sense?"

"Bleach? Why would bleach be...?"

"Right. Ok. Whatever. I'm not bothered. That's enough."

"Why can't I keep my hat? It's the only thing not covered in shit."

"Well that's not my fault is it? You could have gone the park or something."

"You should have left me alone. You didn't have to get involved. Now look at us. All in this state."

"We couldn't leave you alone."

"You leave the other ones alone."

"What other ones? There were no other ones."

"The ones in Crosby. You leave them alone. You let them all just stand there."

"What ones in Crosby?"

"You leave them well alone."

"You weren't in Crosby."

"You leave them alone though."

"I genuinely don't know what you're on about."

"Ask Dave. Ask him how come you leave them alone? The ones in Crosby?"

"I would do but I don't know where he is. He should have been back by now."

"Ask Dave."

"Bloody bursting here."

"Ask him about the ones in Crosby."

"Alright friend, fucking hell, that'll do. I'm not enjoying this, you know. I've got better things. Where is the fat bastard? I'm just about ready to punch someone in the face."

"Well, you can't hit me."

"I know I can't."

"Just so as we are clear. And you can't hit Dave either."

"You're in trouble, you know. You're in bother. You're

45

not here to lay down the law. You don't tell me who I can or can't punch who in the face."

"You're alright, like, but you've got, like, anger issues."

"You've got running around getting covered in shit issues."

"So have you."

"Do you want this punch or not? Do you want my fist to come flying through that beard? Right in the middle of your face?"

"You're funny. Here you are. Here's Dave now. Go on, ask him."

"Bloody hell, Dave! You know what I mean?"

*

"Before I go, I just wanted to say. After before. Don't take this the wrong way, Pauline, but you can't go thinking… There's only so much you can do. First things first, you can't work miracles. Apart from what you did with that, I mean. The thing is, if you think you can it will only make you miserable. Then you'll go off on the Pat and Mick. I've seen it. And that's no good to me.

No good at all. It's no way to run a doodah. You can see how we're fixed otherwise. Believe me."

"I don't really know what you're saying, Paul."

"Like, it doesn't matter. That's all. All you've done is try to help. You just can't always...you know. Stick to what you've been told in your training. We aren't bestowed with the omniscient powers of celestial angels and we're not bleeding robots. That's my motto. Let's face it. It's minimum wage. You do the best you can. If nothing else, someone was there. Then you go home."

"Doesn't feel...you know."

"Well it should. So forget about it. You'll have forgotten about it tomorrow. Guaranteed."

"How do you know all this Paul? How do you manage to make it sound so...?"

"It's the only way to stop yourself cracking up, love."

"If you say so."

"Go on. You'll be fine. I'll be off in a minute if you need me."

*

"Giz a light kid."

"On the vapours, lad, aren't I?"

"This isn't right though, you know."

"Who did he say was after?"

"You heard."

"What the fuck though?"

"Sounded like it anyway. Listen."

"Shh!"

"Here y'are, he's off again."

"Missed it."

"Telling you."

"If you'd shut up, lad..."

"Ask him, lad."

"You ask him."

"Alright. I will."

"No. Don't, lad."

"What?"

"Don't. You can't."

"But..? Hang on, lad."

"I know but...you can't. You don't know what you're doing."

"What do you mean?"

"You can't, lad. That's all."

"You ask him then."

"No what I mean is, you're not trained."

"Are you?"

"No I'm not, lad. That's what I'm saying, lad, you need to be trained."

"Trained for what though?"

"Trained for all this, and that. You know. To deal with things like this. Like dealing with hostages and all that gear."

"Oh behave."

"I'm not messing. This is bang on this is."

"He hasn't got any hostages. Who'd let him take them hostage?"

"I didn't mean like he's got hostages."

"You'd just punch him one. Bang! Snot everywhere.

He's not hard him. All I'll do is, I'm just going to ask him 'what's all this got to do with Peter Gabriel', that's all."

"He might not have actually said Peter Gabriel."

"It sounded like Peter Gabriel."

"I know. I know. It did. Yeah."

"It was you who said he was going on about Peter Gabriel in the first place."

"I know."

"And you're not trained."

"That's the point though. I might be wrong. It might mean...something...else."

"Look. Either he said he wanted to talk to Peter Gabriel and he won't come down until he has or he didn't. The bizzies will be here in a minute. You'll have to tell them something."

"Who will?"

"You will."

"Nah. No way. I'm not talking to them."

"Oh well."

"I'm not telling them that, lad."

"I don't know anything about it. I've only come out for milk."

"They'll think he's a crank."

"They won't."

"Stay with us."

"How long has he been up there?"

"He was already there when I came out. Hang on here. Don't be arlarse. He might fall off."

"What's he got in his bag?"

"He hasn't said."

"How long ago did you phone them?"

"Phone who?"

"You'll have to phone them, lad. Fucking hell. Could be here all day with you."

"They're gonna lock him up aren't they?"

"One of them isn't it?"

"Ah for fuck's sake. I'm not phoning no-one."

"Oh well I don't know."

"Someone else will. Some other nob'ed. And round

here will be crawling. 'Cos of him."

"Don't think, do they?"

"They don't though, do they though?"

"Yeah, alright."

"Divvies."

*

He gets a message from Elvis.

'Thanks for that. I'm still trying to get my head around it. Take it easy and ta for the message mate.'

He walks on towards the river to catch a breeze. He needs to think if there's a better message he can send in return. He needs to think about whether or not he should leave things as they are. It might help him to be near water, to be beside what was there before and will be here after. There is the sound of seabirds as he skirts the Albert Dock, the scatter of electric blue high heels scuttling out of hotels into waiting private hire cabs.

He considers going back to the Tabac to proposition the waitress. He thinks of bringing her here to see the gold upon the water. He imagines the scene.

There'll be a funeral and he doesn't know if he should go. He thinks of taking her along with him. She'd wear a lace mantilla.

He watches the ferry weave its dazzle-ship patterns.

A camera-van has slowed close behind him. He turns and sees there are two uniforms inside. They watch him closely as it passes by. It stops a few yards along, next to the river wall.

His phone goes off again. There's another flashing red mark showing on the map.

*

"Parents, look to your children. Please do not be distracted by my complex oratorical complexities. Let's not beat about the bush here, there's all sorts of oddballs about. And no, I may be unusual, maybe even peculiar but I am not an oddball. I am the most dangerous sort of all. I am a man with an idea. Now draw yourselves closer and have no fear. Come and listen. That's it. Closer. All together, one at a time. For this to work I require a fair bit of your attention. Should it fail I will only have yourselves to blame. Now what we have here under this statue is our very own Speakers Corner. You didn't know that did you? Of course not. Because it wasn't, or isn't, or wasn't until this morning. But here it is. At least, it is now if I have anything to do with it and it seems to my delight and surprise that I have. Got something to do with it. You're all listening aren't you? To me? And I'm standing here. I'm not imagining this am I? I should hope not because if I was I'd have made some of you a little bit better looking, if I'm completely honest with you. I joke of course. You're all extremely gorgeous. Especially you, sir. Haha! But no. Here we are then, ladies and gentleman, and we're lucky enough to be here in Sefton Park in this beautiful sunshine and under a statue exceedingly fair and you're stood there and you're wondering what the heck is going on. Am I right, madam? Of course I am. Well I'm doing what it says on the tin. This is Speakers Corner and I am going to speak. And there you have it. Not hard to follow really is it? What's all the fuss about? Feel free to interject at any moment by the way. I'm not precious about it. I speak. You speak. So long as everybody's happy? I had thought about something I wanted to share this morning and seeing as there's...you have a question, sir? Could you..? The chap over here is kindly and quite rightly enquiring as to when I will be getting on with it. Thankyou for that. I was...until you interrupted but that's perfectly alright. You'll have learnt your lesson I'm sure. So here we go again. I shall proceed forthwith. This is just as hard as I thought, by the way. Anyway. Well here we are. Everyone's paying attention. This is great. This is perfect. I have a question of my own. I have something to share and it's sort of a question. It isn't my question. I just read about it recently. The thing is, and forgive me some of you younger ones, but has everyone here heard of The Beat Generation? You've heard of The Beat Generation? Of course you have. It's where The Beatles got their name. It's all those cool kids back in the fifties and the sixties isn't it? I used to think that The Beat Generation was to do with the beat. It made me think of sharp suits and cool shades, clicky fingers, hip-swivelling jazz moves. Turns out I was dead wrong. Fancy that! It's sometimes quite a wonderful experience to learn that you had gotten everything wrong. You ever really had that? What it was...I found out some time recently that a group of writers, the cool dude types you'd imagine, all 'deal me in daddy-o' and all the rest of it, and they were sat around talking and drinking and smoking the night away and trying to work out what was unique about them, their age and their times. You know how it is. We've all done it. 'What's so...special...about now?' You know. And we know. It's not easy to come up with an answer but that's the point. It isn't meant to be easy. If it was easy... But anyway. One of them speaks up – "I think I've got something" – and everyone leans in and listens. He says that he has noticed how people, these days, they pass by each other on the sidewalks; how rushed and bothered and weary they appear, disinterested with each other, eyes busy but downcast and avoiding contact, no engagement. It's not how he remembers things from when he was a lad, when he'd been a youth. He's gone from a small town to the big city but still. People used to pass the time, or he would say that certainly it used to feel that way. He says he has come to realise that he has seen something similar somewhere else, on a different continent. Those expressions, the body language, that aggravated gait. It reminds him, he says - and he is just realising this as at this moment that he is saying it – it makes him think of the newsreels he had seen along with everyone else, endless reams of footage filmed in the second world war. Those images of broken people, made to feel like bits of nothing, the long enforced marches, trudging along at the side of the road, the poor, defeated, the desolate, with their worldly belongings either lost, destroyed or dragged like so many rags. 'They're beat.', he says. 'They're so burdened and beaten that it takes all their energy to do whatever they have to do. They're done. These people are beat. That's what we've become.' It did my head in, that did, folks. That, just that, when you think about it. I had it completely wrong. The Beat Generation. That's what it was. I was wrong. He said 'this is the beat generation'. Yeah. That was it really. That was about it. That's what I was thinking this morning. I thought it might be worth sharing. I had it all wrong. Yeah. That's what it was. That's it. Yeah. Well, thanks. Yeah, thanks for listening anyway. No, you're alright. I'm ok. I'm…no, I'm fine, honest. No worries. I'm alright. I'll be fine. Don't worry. No, it's ok I've got…yeah, ok, thanks, have you got a light? No honest. No, no need to call anyone. I'll be sound in a minute."

*

Everything that was probably due to him comes to him all at once. The week's post has gathered itself together. There are bailiff letters for debts that he can't remember. The company names on the letterheads are completely unfamiliar. The amounts they demand bear no relation to anything he recalls ever asking for or taking. The last one is the only one he had been expecting; a notice of legal action over unpaid rent. There's some date approaching that must be important. He doesn't read any of the accompanying leaflets. He bunches them up with the torn envelopes and leaves them all together on the ironing board that cuts across the darkest corner of the living room. There are two similar piles that have found themselves behind it on the floor.

He is almost complete.

He plugs the phone into the charger to hear it beep. It hasn't hardly made a sound in days or weeks.

He uses the last drop of milk as he pours another coffee.

He half-fills a plastic bottle with water, shoving it in amongst the pile of dishes and he goes around and splashes a portion on a few of his plants. He half-fills it again and sees to the rest.

He prays in the light of the sun on the spotted speckled carpet.

The only thing in his flat that he is aware of that is in a neat well-attended-to pile is a handful of lottery tickets. Thirty of them, going back at least a couple of months. He has yet to decide if this is the day that he will finally hand them over to be checked. He thinks he possibly fears the process too much again today. He will maybe wait. They have become his only remaining hope of something positive happening and he knows that each time he thinks of it, pictures it, going into the shop, waiting, people waiting in line behind him, knowing, with each and every inevitable disappointment, once they have gone...

He shoves with his bare foot a fallen pile of books up against one of the speakers.

He looks out of the window, over streets and houses,

over grey and guarana-speckled rooftops.

He types:

"Fifty shades of shit and shite #icanseeformiles"

He picks up his phone an hour later. Two retweets. One like. Nowhere near good enough really. It hadn't been worth it.

*

Within half an hour McKelnikov is breaching the top of Myrtle Street. He walks through the railway park towards the houses at the top of the hill. He can see the people gathered, a few more than earlier with kids out circling on small-wheeled brightly-coloured pushbikes. He pulls down his cap slightly, roughens up his beard and makes his way towards them. This one doesn't look very different from the other: half-length grey shorts, dark blue t-shirt, face the same, expression the same, there but not there. Blank. Like a ship's lookout without a ship.

A woman is standing with her arms crossed while a policeman waits at her side with a notebook.

"Like his father. Exactly like him.'

'What might he have taken, love?"

"He's in Sweden last I heard. He's not interested."

He nods as if he understands. The young lad remains unmoved. A slight breeze flicks at the sleeves of his t-shirt. He sits on the sloping grey tiles, his legs stretched straight with the heels of the souls of his trainers clipped against the guttering. He has his hands pressed down to keep himself still. He settles on his back and looks up at the sky. A teenager on the street is filming in circles around himself.

McKelnikov decides to move onward. He walks to the top of the lane and turns back on himself down Upper Parliament Street. The houses are out of view from the main road.   A few cars pass by in small bunches. Nobody would know anything was happening. When he blinks he allows in his mind's eye flashes, visions; of barricades and flames, shouts and charges, of slow-moving images from newspaper photographs, still jerked frozen black and white moments of confrontation. Headlines that tell of the 'The Last Days of the Rialto'.

He feels the heat of the fire. His mouth drying out. Almost choking heat.

*

"Still don't know what I've been…waiting for."

"…"

"What?"

"Go on."

"Just singing to myself."

"Is this all her idea?"

"Don't start all that again."

"They won't do anything, you know. Just cos…at the end of the day…"

"Okay. Let me work out where we are meant to be. Less chatter. More thingy. What's the street?"

"This is it here, right here, bear right. Spot on. You can't blame…"

"I'll blame who I want. Who'd be arsed with it anyway?"

"You've got the wrong end of the stick."

"Alright."

"Yeah."

"Sound."

"That's what I'm saying."

"Nice one."

"Ok then."

"Alright."

"So what are you going to do?"

"Fuck off, I suppose. That's what happens isn't it? You go and live somewhere else. She's done it. Now it's my turn. That's how it goes. It does happen, as you very well know. Anyway, this will do us. Helmets on, boys, there's ladies present."

"Ladder job."

"Looks like it."

"Three wire?"

"About that."

"Two or three?"

"Probably get away with two."

"Could maybe do with bringing it back a couple of yards."

"This is fine."

"Little bastard. Look at the cut of him. What is it? He

on the dark side of the moon, do you reckon?"

"Ah well. Keeps us busy. It's all work. Bread and butter, boys. Shoes for the kids, and that. Don't knock it."

*

The Tabac looks too busy for him now: a few uninterested faces inside looking out and the waitress in constant movement. He passes the steps of St Luke's as a group of grey-skinned grey-clothed men huddle and muddle into each other as the lips of a plastic bottle fizzes and spills over sleeves and fingers. The heat is beginning to radiate from sun-blasted walls. The brighter air thickens as he looks and blinks down the length of Bold Street. He steps into a shop and buys the cheapest looking bottle of water. Further on he finds himself opening the door to the Oxfam. He is met by the push of a smell that while not distinctly unpleasant is not particularly pleasing either - of furniture polish fighting against rot - and deafeningly still swirls of sparkling dust dance in and out of nowhere. The front section is given over to dark wooden bookshelves divided into fiction, non-fiction, plays, poetry, reading guides, travel guides, atlases, colouring books, childrens' books, local history, British history, military history, world history. The far end is mostly second hand clothes and stage-wear. Dead men's shoes and blazers. There's a wedding dress in the window with slightly yellowed dropped shoulders perfectly fitted to a headless mannequin. A woman in her sixties has appeared from the store-room and is heaving herself into a washed-out pink mackintosh. She addresses an older woman who follows her dutifully to the till.

"This is it, She. That's what I'm saying. He's a nuisance. I've had to send for an Uber."

When the door closes behind her, the other woman shrugs to nobody in particular.

"It was hardly worth her coming in. Hey ho, the wind and the rain."

She sees him looking over at her from over by the cd's.

"I like 'Clare du Lune' myself. I love the way it goes."

He clears his throat but can't think of a response. She looks at him helpfully.

"Debussy. We haven't got it. I've looked. I can put it to one side if it comes in? We do *do* that."

"Ok. Thanks."

She straightens her glasses and looks around the desk.

"I'll just make a note of it for myself and I can leave it for Elaine and Marion and Marie."

*

"How did it go?"

"Alright."

"Go on?"

"No. It was. It was alright."

"Did anyone listen?"

"A few yeah. Oh yeah there were a few."

"How many?"

"Oh about twenty. Fifteen or twenty. Maybe twenty."

"That's good then?"

"It's alright."

"That's great. Twenty."

"It's not bad."

"And what did you talk about?"

"It doesn't matter."

"No go on. I want to hear."

"It was nothing really. I spoke but I suppose I was hoping that we'd talk about it, that there might be a response or something, but they only listened. I don't know. Maybe I'm not all that good at it."

"It'll take time. You've got to get used to it. I wouldn't have the bottle. No way. Go on. Tell us about it. I wish I'd been there now. Will you tell me next time?"

"I don't know if I..."

"Why not?"

"I'm not sure. That's all."

"Go on. Tell us what you talked about. This is boss. 'Speakers Corner'. I love it."

"It's a good idea, like."

"Oh yeah. Deffo!"

"I just don't know if anyone else will, you know, jog in."

"I reckon they will. You can't expect, your first go... Anyway, I think it's brilliant."

"It's alright, isn't it? As an idea, and that?"

"It is. It's ace. I'm made up for you."

"It's not really my idea. It's from London really."

"I'm proud of you, babe. What have you had to eat? I've took chops out."

*

"You'd better tell him, lad."

"Nah."

"Serious."

"No way, lad. No chance. No way though. I'm not telling him."

"Lad, he's had it, lad."

"Who said, lad? And who said he's a grass?"

"It's on you, kid. If you don't…"

"You don't even know what's thingy."

"Lad, I do my own thing, I know nothing about nothing. You know how it is."

"How much does he owe? Grands?"

"Nah not grands."

"So what's to do with them?"

"I don't know. They're just onto him. They've got him down as being bang at the bollocks."

"I'm not telling him. I'm just not."

"He's your mate."

"He'll go berzerk. He'll shit himself."

"They'll boot his head up and down the street like a casey."

"For all I know…"

"They'll drive a fucking great big four by four jeep through his Ma's house, right through the bay window and they'll park up in the middle of her living room where the couch used to be and they'll fuck with the telly so she's only got Freeview."

"He hasn't even done nothing!"

"They reckon he has though. They reckon he's been looking for a crop and he's either found theirs and taxed it or he's told someone and took a bit of a drink."

"How do they know it was anything to do with him?"

"Cos he's known for it, that's why. Behave."

"People are onto it now. They don't even put them in the loft."

"Some do. One of their boys did. And his back door's gone in, hasn't it? On the road behind his. What do you reckon? Just telling you the Bobby Moore, that's all."

"Alright, I'll have a fucking word."

"Go ed. Tell him to go to their kids' caravan or something."

"They jibbed him off after Christmas. All the prezzies and that."

"Well, wherever. Amsterdam or something."

"As if. He'd have to bunk the bus to the airport."

"Up to him, lad. Just telling you. One of them, lad. That's all."

"Go on then."

"Go on, lad. I'll let you go."

*

Once he is outside he takes off his hat and puts on his shades. He heads to Church Street. Back to what he is supposed to be doing. Tuning in. There are more people around, all the more for him to look at. Splodges and streams of people ducking in and out of shops. Everything gathered in the town: the things that need the people, the people who need the things.

He needs the people. He needs them so that he can watch.

He is part of everything and nothing. At once he is conscious of being broken away from a conspiracy but somehow still he is permitted to observe.

He is grateful for having his mind taken away from what he should or shouldn't be saying to Elvis.

Perhaps he should tell him, gently, in person, that it never really gets all that much better and there'll be times when you aren't certain but you suspect that you would swap everything you have, and ever will have, for one more day in her company and not necessarily a day back then but right now would do, with you as you are and her however she wants to be, wherever she'd want to be.

You suspect that if you were offered, if it was possible, you would give everything.

He decides that it is becoming too hot, too insufferably

overwhelmingly...

He stops and takes a gulp from his bottle. The water splashes at the corners of his mouth and onto the shoulders of his t-shirt.

He checks his position for the cameras.

He checks the position of the sun. Wherever he is, the sun is. Where he goes, it goes. It stays.

He is beginning to wonder. What's up with the sun?

*

"Have you read these comments?"

"I was just about to."

"I think you'd better read them now."

"Why the panic? Sorry, not panic. I just meant...sorry."

"Oh the usual lunatics, that's all. But it needs sorting asap."

"On mine?"

"On all of them. Not all of them. Some of them. Enough of them. Just check your own."

"Why do they bother?"

"Same old story."

"How do you mean?"

"Something to do, I suppose."

"It's got their names on though? They should be reported."

"Who to?"

"You know… Actually, I don't know. Can they be reported?"

"If it's bad, if it's really bad. Not all of them have their names on anyway."

"Here you go. This one here. 'Same old Echo with its multiculture bullshit, give it a rest' – Marie Evans. 'Arabs' – spelt with two r's and two b's– followed by half a dozen question marks."

"Keep going. There's spam or adverts or something further down."

"Bloody buggers."

"Nothing you can do."

"There must be some way we can stop these other ones as well? They're so ignorant."

"If it wasn't for the cranks probably nobody would write anything. How many of these 15 things have you pinched from last week, by the way?"

"Just a couple."

"And the next post? Is it ready?"

"Nothing's really happened yet?"

"There's always something, Lorna. Let's not get stupid about it and lazy. Last thing you want yourself to look like is lazy. I'm not saying you are but you're still on trial yet. If nothing's happening you can't just sit there, you have to think what needs to be said about what isn't happening, you know, instead, or what might be happening. There's always something to... It's just, you take your eye off the ball in this game and you're finished in this game."

"I understand."

"Think on."

"Thanks. I appreciate it."

"No problem. Well done. What time is it? Ok. Good. So what we'll do is..."

"I might do something on Donald Trump."

"Cool. Do that. I'll check on it later. You crack on here.

I'll be in my office. Right. Good. Ok. That's...yeah.
Ok."

*

He thinks he recognises one of a pair of women who are
making straight from the bus for Primark. He follows
them to the door. It isn't who he thought it was. He
counts a beat as he lets them go and he turns the
corner quickly, feeling shorter of breath, heading into
the front yard of the Bluecoat. The doors have not yet
opened so he sits at a wooden table. He takes a drink,
looks again at his phone and opens up the map. He
sees four glowering red dots. One is Upper Frederick
Street. One is Smithdown Lane. The third is around a
mile and a quarter away and looks like it is moving,
somewhere along the near end of Park Road heading
towards him. He feels like he is trapped. He is stuck in
town and needs to move out. He imagines what is
happening on the estates. The scenes blur and merge
together...

There's a clump of figures ahead.

There's the shapes. The skylines.

The young men remain unshifted.

Patrol bikes. Dark blue Astras.

He moves in closer:

He sees dark blue suits. Men talk amongst themselves. One turns away and opens a gate, walks up a path and seems to say something to the lad up above. After a few moments he glides inside, leaving the door open, he can watch through a gap in the crowd as the suit inspects a couple of rooms, stops and stands halfway down the hall talking to someone. When he comes back out he goes straight to his colleagues. He shrugs an expected disappointment.

He tries to work out the conversation that might have taken place -

They, whoever is inside, either can't give or refuses to have any influence.

Everything rests on a sort of gentleness.

He tries to decide where all this comes from - something he has heard or read or seen, unreal and real but he knows it from somewhere.

A lad. A lad on a roof.

Manchester. Or in the Bronx.

Top floor of a multi-storey car park, town centre. Or the flat roof of a brownstone.

Paul Newman with his hat on backwards, acting the goat.

Stood there one minute talking to me like I'm talking to you.

The right and the wrong tone of voice.

Six ambulances. Five of them for witnesses.

"You can't help feeling you could have done more."

"Th-th-th-that's all folks!"

That's showbiz.

*

The Blarney Stone is a sozzler's pub. It has changed hands and names over the years but it has never been anything more than it is now. It is, to put it most simply, New Boots 'n' Panties come to life. A place where Copperas Hill Gene Vincents buy drinks for Mount Pleasant Patricias, where blonde hair turns to old gold and dark is dyed black. The karaoke starts at lunchtime and there's a permanent whisky and orange haze.

"Go 'ed. Two pairs of pints and a large White for the arl

girl. A large small one if she can't hear me. Stick our Francis down for Suspicious Minds or he'll only moan, when you're ready."

On the wall behind the bar is a selection of used banknotes from around the world. The mirrors are all brown-liquor branded. Hand-sized alternate lime-green and sick-yellow stars ziggle prices across the worn-wood head-high glass rail. There is a sign pointing a black-gloved hand with an outstretched fore-finger to a beer garden out at the back. It isn't a beer garden, it's a smoke garden. It isn't a garden. It's a tightly cluttered yard. There is another sign beside it asking patrons to kindly refrain from standing out front by the bus stop. Anyone found breaking this rule and worrying the students will be at least temporarily barred by strict order of the landlord.

It's a pub that always seems to be on a low crackle. When the doors are opened there's a thirst outside, sanctuary inside. There are good days and better days but everything essentially remains the same. All are equal. There is no pretense. Everything is visible. Lunchtimers let on to afternoon-heads. Some stay into the evening. Everyone has found themselves home by the end of the night. Nerves are firmly settled. A pub that's just so, and so, and when all of a sudden someone bursts in through the doors like in what was later described as 'a scene from a crap Western' everyone turns to see. Eddie Ed-rest was doing his

Jealous Guy, Tony Bluebottle was at the ready to give it Where the Streets Have No Name. Or it could have been the other way around – either way, one of them was interrupted (and later kept going on and on about it like that's all that mattered). Glasses at rest were brought within reach, conversations halted. The lad everyone was watching stops still in the middle of the bar, a space clearing around him, a look of increasing panic in his eyes. On his wrists are clearly to be seen a pair of silver handcuffs. Everyone looks at them. They're not the fancy kind. There's nothing kinky about him. Let there be no doubt. He stares at them himself for a moment, then he bolts for the back door. People are getting up from their seats. Something of a murmur is rising up, someone sensing themselves elected with a series of nods to follow him out.

In the cold-shadowed yard he paces around within the handful of smokers, forcing a circle for himself as they step back out of his way, their glasses protectively held to their chests. His feet stomp, eyes frantically searching out a solution. He sees inspiration in a stool that offers him a foothold up onto the top of a steel barrel. He overbalances on the rim and falls sideways to the ground. There's a collective "woah there lad" as a couple of the men reach down to help him to his feet. A woman steps forward to brush his sleeve and his cheek free of dirt and grit and a folded ciggy butt. She looks for a handkerchief in her handbag. He pushes them all away and rolls himself sideways onto the table. Empties are lifted as he scrambles to his knees and onto his feet. He scrapes the link between his handcuffs against the corner brickwork, releasing a long futile moaning whimper, his hands out pleadingly before him. He grips onto a drainpipe, finds a ledge for one foot and levers himself upward. He does the same again using the outer wall to get him to the next level. He gets higher, moving across to a first floor window, voices below reaching up to him. Their words are mixed with laughter. He looks down. They see his pale blank frozen fear. They quieten for a moment. He pulls himself further away. There's a groan as he scales to the next ledge, then laughter again. He pulls at the drainpipe and sees that it is strong enough to take all of his slight weight. He doesn't look down again, he keeps on going. He keeps escaping.

*

"I know. I've just seen him."

"Who was it?"

"Their Margaret's lad."

"It hasn't been on the news."

"Why? What's this you're watching?"

"Housewives. The New York. I've got a Mob Wives. And I've got an Atlanta."

"You've watched New York."

"Have I?"

"You know you have."

"Oh well. You've been ages. Who else is out there?"

"Here we go."

"Anyone I know?"

"Go and have a look, nose disease."

"Is Michaela there?"

"I didn't see her."

"Is Our Becca?"

"I didn't look."

"What about Mandy?"

"What about her?"

"You're no use. I'll look on the Whatsapp. What's he doing up there anyway?"

"Nothing."

"Nothing?"

"Literally nothing. Just sat there on the roof. He was shouting all sorts earlier but there's not a peep out of him now. He went quiet once they turned up."

"Who?"

"Coppers. Fire bobbies. The lot. Everyone. All the carry-on."

"His poor mother. What was she doing?"

"I didn't see her."

"Typical. It's all over Facebook."

"What's it say?"

"Why are they all going on about Phil Collins? He's not dead is he?"

"What do you mean?"

"I don't know."

"No. Bloody hell, girl. It's the other one. The Sledgehammer fella."

"Oh. Well what about him?"

"He can't stay up there forever. He'll need a crap at

some point."

"Derek!"

"He will though.   He could have a piss behind the chimney pot. But if he wants a Tom Tit he's had it. Just being practical, that's all. You can't just go off half cock. So what did it say in the Echo?"

"Nothing really. 'Road closed blah blah'. Nothing much. People were writing all sorts of horrible comments on the Echo."

"Cranks."

"I know."

"Weirdos."

"I know."

"Did you write anything?"

"Just that it's a nice area and people shouldn't go judging everything, you know, like the way people do. It's not all like him. It used to be nice."

"Is there anything on the Sky Arts?"

"Yeah, I'll have a look shall I?"

"Or the Mob Wives. It's up to you."

"No go on it's up to you."

"I'm happy with either. What's up with that fella on Cheaters? You might as well delete all of them. He's ruined that programme."

"Clark Gable would be turning in his grave."

"Something not right about that fella."

"Gives me the creeps."

"I'll stick the kettle on, shall I? No danger of drowneding round here is there?"

"I've got someone coming later."

"Alright, I'll keep myself out the way."

"Thanks, love."

"No problem. Got a couple of eclairs here as well."

"Yers. They'll go with a cup of tea."

"Exactly what I was thinking."

"Did they have the sticker on though?"

"They'll be fine. They'll be gone in five minutes."

*

Police have followed him into the pub. The music has run out on its own. Two uniforms go into the back as two remain standing in the middle of the bar trying not to look uncomfortable. A few faces are too easily recognised. Everyone pretends not to be looking so closely at one another. The two return and take the others onto the street. Drinkers move to the window and chuckle and cheer as they watch them stepping into the traffic, to the opposite side, all the while looking up to the tops of the buildings. One of them points! They are peering and staring - a bus goes past and blocks the view – and when they reappear there is a clear alarm, and jeering laughter inside at the silent pushing and pulling at each other on the outside, the policemen moving both left and right at the same time. A dark hard missile crashes against a wall behind them. Uproar! Another breaks into fragments on the concrete a few feet away. The policemen split both ways.

Maureen phones to upstairs and tells Deanne to wake up Gerry. She tells her again, sternly this time, quietly, with her back to everyone. A few seconds later he is bounding down blurry-eyed, pushing through from behind the bar as he tucks his white shirt into the waistband of his black pants, pushing up the sleeves, expecting to hit somebody immediately but there is no-one facing up to him for a fight. Regulars close in with a gaggled explanation, his eyes narrowing as he listens. His mood visibly moves from bitterness to weariness.

He looks to Maureen but she can merely shrug her agreement. He goes out into the back. His expression demands that something be done but the smokers take both sides.

"They can't climb after him, Gerry. Fucking hell, lad."

"You'll have them all fall down."

"Are you insured for this kind of caper?"

"I wouldn't fancy a dance with our kid up there, would you?"

"Four floors of fucking about."

"For a kick off."

"He's off his bonce, Gerry."

"You're best leave him."

He is called inside. A senior officer wants to speak to him. He goes out and lets the doors close behind him.

"You'll have to.', he is told.

"This is fucking great this is. Fucking brilliant. Fucking smart like. Boss!"

"You want me to do it?"

"You want a shit cunt of a riot? I'll frigging do it."

When he comes back in they can all tell the impending bad news immediately from the look on his face.

"Ah go'way Gerry."

"Come on. You know the score. Towel's on. Everyone out."

"Fuck off, Gerry lad!"

"Leave him up there."

"He'll come down when he's ready."

"If he jumps, he jumps."

"And if he doesn't, no harm done."

"He's pulling our roof apart brick by brick.", Maureen bites back.

"Tile by tile.", someone corrects her.

Someone is watching at the window as another crash is heard.

"It's like 9/11 out there, lad."

"OUT!", shouts Gerry. "I've had e-fucking-nough of this."

*

I was asked what I know about it.

I'm asked specifically about the ones that they say have been going up onto rooftops. The police haven't given them much to go on and there's nothing that has come their way that could be described as a psychiatric assessment. It's early days. Or early doors, as he called it. He gives me a brief run down, describing the ones they know about so far but it's hardly worth it to be honest. There really isn't enough...substance, let alone anything you could call useful data.

He said he was from the Liverpool Echo, which I presume is the main paper in the area. I wouldn't know. I've been to Manchester a few times. But he sounded very young. He said he got my name from google. I'm not sure I understand how. I really should have asked, just out of interest, to see how these things work.

He said that they are all men, of course, and that they're between twenty and fifty years of age. They're all white men, if that makes a difference. I said it might.

He said they are climbing up and sitting on rooftops.

None of them are saying anything of any use and most aren't saying anything at all.

None of them appear to be connected but there has to be something they have in common. I guess that's why he called me. To try to find out if there was some sort of recognised...thing. I didn't want to disappoint him. Professionally, I sort of had to say something.

"One reason could be that they have serious mental health issues going on, so it could be a cry for attention, as they know the emergency services will come out. Or it could be a power issue because they know that once they get up there they're going to be commanding the police who will have to go into critical incident management. Or it could be Contagion Theory coming into play. We see that happen when there's a suicide. If people who are depressed and have got suicidal ideation, ideas, yes, they see somebody else doing it, it creates this influx. Or it could be that people who are on the run from police and are anti-social in some way have seen people running up onto rooftops in the media and think 'that's a good idea'. It could be something like that. It's dependent on the individual case but because they've seen it and... they know it's one way to get a lot of exposure and cause a lot of grief to the police. They'll get arrested in the end anyway – just after causing a lot of fuss. It is certainly an interesting phenomenon as you describe it. How many have you got so far did you say?"

You don't always know where these things might lead. I presume there must be local TV and radio as well but it didn't seem appropriate to ask him. I do think it's something I should add to my profile though, you know, just in case. He did say I'd definitely have my name in the article. It should be available soon. I'll send you the link. I'm hoping it will be tomorrow!

*

"We've got one going on about Peter Bloody Frigging Gabriel who I don't even know if he is still alive."

"He is, sir."

"Great. I was joking. We've got one on top of his nan's sticking two fingers up. Where's he? Yeah that one. Charming. We've got those two you said. There's this one on Renshaw."

"There's two more, sir."

"Three more."

"Right. How many have we actually got?"

"I've got nine."

"I've got ten."

"Is that ten in total? Or is it nineteen? What do you mean? Who is co-ordinating all of this?"

"This is it, sir."

"This is it? So, nothing so far?"

"Nothing really at all."

"You needn't look so smug about it. This is supposed to be a handover."

"Beyond my purview all this, sir."

"Cunt."

"Should we maybe pinpoint them on a map?"

"Good idea."

"And then, maybe…"

"What?"

"There might be a pattern."

"Fuck me. Another cunt."

"No I just mean…"

"What's it going to spell out? A pentagram or something? The name of the mystery killer?"

"Sorry, sir."

"Bleeding Barnaby over here."

"No I meant...I don't know, sir."

"We're not pissing about here, ladies and gentleman. Now speak up, please. Someone, speak to me now. Please! Someone sober. Something. Anything. Ok. Fucking hell. Let's think. Ok. Right. For fuck's sake. Get them all up on the bastard board. On the map. Like on the telly. Come on. Do that at least. Do the map thing like he says. Let's make some bloody sense of it. Hurry up, come on. Let the dog see the rabbit. Is there anything there at all? Come on idiots, someone give me an answer to something. Jesus wept! All I need this on a fucking Sunday."

"Some aren't saying anything. The ones who are..."

"It's all broken biscuits."

"There's only one who has got any demands."

"Demands? No-one said..."

"Lad in Walton, sir, wants twenty Lambert and Butler and a Dominos before he'll come down off his arl fella's."

"And that's what you call a demand is it? Not exactly 'I want a jet plane, take me to fucking Cuba' is it?"

"It's not ISIS anyway. At least we know that."

"Depends. What does he want on his pizza?"

"And the others...fuck all, I suppose?"

"The one on the pub was in the middle of being nicked for acting suspiciously in the off license round the corner."

"Oh aye?"

"What he was doing, sir, I don't know, sir, but he's jumped out of the car when he's seen his chance and he's pegged it."

"Doesn't make sense either though does it? You try to escape you don't go up. There's only so far up you can go. You stay on the horizontal and try to get further away don't you? Am I mad? I'm right aren't I? Away is good. Up is shit. I'm just saying, sir. Basic."

"None of them makes sense. You don't just go and sit on a fucking roof. We've had rooftops for hundreds, fucking thousands of years and it's on my billet, on my shift when I'm on call-out that these scumbags decide they all need sitting on? Well, balls to that. They can all fuck off. And you can tell them that. Have any of them jumped? Do any of them know each other?"

"Not as far as we know, sir."

"And how many negotiators have we got?"

"You're looking at them."

"You two?

"Us two."

"Two on duty?"

"Two full stop."

"I've done a bit of a course."

"We'll need bodies. What are we looking for?"

"People with nice voices?"

"Come on, now, let's stop this pissing about. We'll need a fucking great big think here. Hold off with putting any of this on the news. Copycats and...I don't know. They can stick their Twitter up their arse."

"Exactly."

"Who would want to copy this though?"

"Fuck knows. But keep it to a minimum until we know what's going on. Come on. Pull your frigging fingers out, pardon my French. So far we don't know anything. Go and get talking to them. To their mothers. Neighbours. Whoever. Give us a bastard clue. And don't think I'm satisfied, don't think it has gone unnoticed that you've all done just about the square root of fuck all while you were waiting for me. Someone should have been onto this from the twat-faced start. I'm not happy with this...this shower of shit. On a Sunday. Jesus. This isn't good. You may have noticed that this isn't what we want, children. Ok? Is it getting through to you? And if you have noticed that this isn't what we want you could maybe do something about it. Make it better. Not worse. I am not a particularly happy man. And you are a shower of shite. The lot of you. Now get on with it. Now! Go! NOW!!! Fucking arseholes."

*

The policeman stationed at the door leans out and looks in turn from left to right.

"We'll go left. Come on, folks, that'll do now, off we jolly well go.", he says finally. "Stay close to the wall if you don't want your head sliced clean off like the top of a jelly, there's lovely."

Movement in the room is minimal. Everyone looks set firm where they sit or stand. Some are going back to their conversations.

"I won't say it again!"

There are a few confused looks.

"Where are you from, lad?"

"Have you been sent to save us?"

"Come on. This is an incident. Shift yourselves ladies and gentlemen if you please."

He focusses on the tables nearest to him, each taken by a man or woman aged somewhere between seventy and forever: blazers and trousers, mac and handbag, brylcreem grey and curler-black hair, tape-repaired spectacles, folded smudged newspapers.

"Come on Dad. And you missus. Up we get. That'll do."

A couple of younger men pick up their pints and poke their heads out. They gesture that there are more police on the corners. One of them steps all the way out. There's a grumbling acceptance as the rest begin to collect themselves and what they need and accept the disruption. Maureen carefully locks the till and puts the key inside her bra. Gerry reaches behind the karaoke machine and flicks switches at the wall. Deanne slips in with the others as they allow themselves to be ushered towards the door but all movement is halted. There's a blustering look on the face of the lad as he returns to tell them:

"Here! You can't take your ale out."

"What did you say, Kev? What did you say lad?"

"They said...you'll have to put it in a plastic glass."

Maureen's shoulders sag. Her groan is drowned out by all the others.

"Fucking hell!"

"It's not my fault", she says as she passes them out. She is told to pour herself a large Dissaranno and does so, first into a brandy glass and then into an emptied teacup. She drinks it all down and puts her handbag over her shoulder. Gerry jangles keys behind to hurry them all up. She puts her hand above her head like she has seen in the films and crouches as she walks. There's all shouting:

"It's the fall of Saigon all over again."

"Shut up and stay by the wall!"

She sees a couple of dozen smashed slates scattered like outbreaks of acne.

"Oh Tilly, love, come on out of the way. Give us your hand."

As they turn the corner they both get their breaths back.

"Everyone was having such a nice time. Oh how they

love to ruin it."

"I know, love."

"You can't have nothing, Maureen. It's selfish."

"We're alright here."

"I don't care what anyone says."

Maureen puts an arm around her. They hear Gerry catch up behind them.

"Tony! Go and get your airgun, lad."

They all sense the startled stare and discomfort of the young policeman stood as sentry on the corner.

"I'm joking. I'm only bloody joking aren't i? I'm allowed to make a joke of it. It is my bleeding roof! This is costing me money. You're on your overtime. You're bloody made up!"

*

"You live your life in a fantasy.", she said. "Your head is full of all this nonsense and you pretend that everything is okay, that it will turn out fine, but it isn't okay, it's not okay. You aren't dealing with reality."

And she was right about everything. She was then and she is now. It isn't okay. Everything isn't okay, with me, with everyone else, with me dealing with everyone else...

I could have been a negotiator. I'm calm, mostly, and reassuring, mostly. But I don't know if I'd care. They'll come down when they're ready. They're just there. And they say only three out of ten are talked down anyway. They'll come down when it goes dark, before it gets terrifying. We all know that. They're mad but they will come down. But the thing is, all the same, there's something not right. Someone will have to do something.

The sun doesn't move much at all when you watch it this closely.

I might have felt differently before but I can't remember. I used to think a lot about the future. I used to think about it too much. I used to use my imagination a lot more than I do now. Things would be eventually be alright in there. I could imagine everything actually being alright.

But I don't like things as much as I used to. I'd prefer a good sleep, a really really good one, but it's difficult to get hold of. You know.

Nothing is actually now anymore. It's all gone all flat.

I can't see it, can't see out of it. This incredible anguish.

I don't want anything.

I don't want any more.

I wouldn't describe any of this to Gerry. I wouldn't want to bother Maureen with any of it either.

Can you hear what they are saying? I can't hear anything anymore. I can't hear anything over the sound of the helicopter.

When did that thing appear? It looks fantastic from below. It must look even better from inside it.

*

Gerry is fuming. Maureen worries within herself that he might finally be right.

She stands in the shadows and draws deeply on a cigarette. She wonders at people. She hears things, in the things that they say.

Tilly listens. She is distracted but she is listening.

"'How are you Jacks?' I say. 'Up the wall', she'll say back. Bloody hell. 'How's it going Mary?', 'Oh don't

99

ask, Mo, they've got me demented'. I don't know. 'I've got everyone going bananas at me'. He's on this, she's on that. I don't know when everything went so...stupid. I used to say to him, I used to say "Gerry, don't be a misery, give them their due, they're having a go'. Not any more. There's nothing left, nothing left to...nothing left to say. Everyone has gone mental."

"You don't know what goes on." answers Tilly. She watches as the other customers head around towards The Vines.

"Too many secrets." says Maureen finally. "Or something."

"I know."

"Too much...I don't know."

"It's one of them."

Maureen looks intently at her, irritated.

"One of what, Tilly? That's all anyone ever says. What's it supposed to actually mean?"

"I don't know. Don't pick on me. I haven't climbed up anything. Not for donkey's years."

Maureen goes into her bag for her packet of fags. She fishes one out and hands it to Tilly.

"Ah stay and have a smoke with me, Till. Don't go just yet. I'm rattled aren't I? I'm all over the place. You can't blame me. We might be out here forever."

The older woman takes a look around. There are only a handful of the men still in conference with Gerry where nobody else can hear them.

"Let's go the Vines. Let's go and see Cathy. It'll all be alright. Gerry is here. Come on. This is depressing."

They link arms and walk together around the corner.

"Let the men sort it out.", she says and they both share the same dry laugh.

*

"Right."

"So."

"We're agreed."

"Undoubtedly."

"Something has happened."

"Something's going on out there now that wasn't going

"on before."

"In some way."

"It's like the Anthony Gormley gone wrong."

"Or David Essex in the War of the Worlds."

"Only he wanted to live underground."

"That's right. He built a cricket pitch didn't he? That was it. Hospitals and…"

"Yeah that's super. Thanks. Anyway. Focus! By the way, I agree. They can't all be different."

"What are we going to do if they are?"

"No. I'm not having it. They can't all have just decided…no way."

"How are we supposed to put this together without talking to anyone?"

"I know. I'm with you. But you heard. We can't. Got to give it a wide berth."

"They don't want anything in."

"Only the basics."

"So you can only sketch it out."

"Talk to people anyway."

"Got to."

"Just be discreet."

"The mothers.   The emergency services.   The neighbours."

"They won't know anything."

"Local shopkeepers.   They know what's up with everyone."

"Anyone else will just say they don't know what's come over them.   All we've got so far is 'salt of the earth, wouldn't harm a fly' rubbish."

"Are we...are we sure this is really happening?"

"What do you mean?"

"It's just... Yeah, I don't know what I mean.   It's just weird."

"Is it though?"

"Isn't it?"

"I don't know."

"It is happening a bit.   There's the pictures."

"Why now though?"

"That's what's so...   That's what I don't get."

"I know but... I don't know."

"There must be something."

"Nothing heavy goes in til we get the go ahead but in the meantime we work something up, something, or we might as well not be here, we could all be at home staring at the wall doing nothing."

"Working title: 'why are men in Liverpool going up on rooftops?'"

"Merseyside."

"Oh alright."

"Wool."

"Til then it's just...you know, traffic news."

"They're onto it anyway on the social media. Have a look. It's pointless trying to pretend."

"Yeah well, we'll do as we're told."

"I'm not happy with this stuff from the psychologist. Hardly expert opinion is it? Who phoned him?"

"I did. And it was a her. And she didn't really have anything to say, to be honest. That's everything. Said there isn't a name for it. And if they're all different. End of. But anyway, it was all news to her. I was like, even if they were freaking out somehow, how come they weren't doing this before? They weren't doing this a year ago. How come they aren't doing it anywhere else?"

"What did she say?"

"She went quiet for a bit and then she asked me if we were still going to pay her."

"How much did you offer?"

"£150."

"And are you going to? For that?"

"He'll have to. Unless there's anything else we can use."

"Find another one. No offence, but…"

"We'll have to print something. We'll look well if something mad happens and we haven't even got three hundred words."

*

The landlady of The Vines is at the nearest point of the bar. She is half-hanging over in anticipation. She is delightedly concerned as they both walk in.

"Oh Maureen, thank god you're alright love, come over here, come on, let me see you're ok, god love you. How are you Tilly, love? It's terrible. Shocking. Have a brandy. A large brandy. And pass Tilly a half of Guinness. I can't believe it."

The regulars of the Blarney are sharing their views with the regulars of the Vines.

"Is right though."

"Should be happy with a pint."

"That's where they're all going ske-wiff."

"There's too many. Just far too many."

"It's nature. I've said it before."

"What you don't do, what you definitely don't do, is climb on a roof."

"That's the last thing you want to do."

"You just get on with it."

"What goes up..."

"He's right."

"Only one place you're going."

"Broad Oak."

"Or Stothart."

"Never, ever, would you ever, ever, never would you catch me in a million billion years…"

They all look to Maureen.

"And I'm meant to be the one with a few slates missing."

"You know what you could do with, Mo?", asks Cathy. Everyone silently freezes.

"Another brandy?"

"A night on the tiles."

Gerry enters. Everyone else but he, Maureen and Cathy are in the midst of warm laughter. He tries to not look uncomfortable. He has the walk of the not particularly welcome. He whispers in Maureen's ear. He makes only a fleeting eye contact with Cathy and they avoid the embarrassment of a greeting.

No, he says, don't worry, he isn't going to do anything silly.

Cathy quietly despairs of it all despite how she appears. She thinks of this as some sort of high minded low living. Better to have things out in the open, she thinks, but other people aren't like that. So everybody suffers.

For Maureen, a slow riot is breaking out all around her and has been for a while. She has been around town for too long not to know when something dangerous is happening.

She thinks. Cathy thinks.

Romantically, to the verge of insanity.

I shall die of this, they are both thinking.

We will all laugh ourselves to death as we go along with it all, like it's all some wretched duty, like we are all lambs entirely.

Gerry can't answer for the entirety of it. He is only one man. He can only be himself. This is about how they themselves are feeling.

Change was not going to be enough. It's just change. And things always stay the same.

It needs to rain. Or it needs to go dark.

Tilly is sat at a table talking quietly and conspiratorially to a woman her own age. They stop when they see Cathy looking over. Maureen sighs but she joins them anyway.

*

All I wanted to do was to point at this thing.

A sad gypsy serenades the moon. It's all as crap as all that.

If we had a bullring, a coliseum...

If a man can't tell us what he means:

let's presume that his words must have a meaning beyond utterance

and are merely misunderstood,

and that his incoherence

and inevitable intolerability

fools us into thinking

he is doing something fine.

We are behaving too well, sometimes, when all is chaos, and rapid sensation, with no discernible centre, when nothing is all that clear at all.

This feeling of being both a slave and a master, reduced to chucking the china about and insulting everyone.

I have not even eaten. There is nothing I would prefer.

There doesn't always have to be a dagger scene, not

always, but we do have to have a mad one. To make sense of it all. The fine thing is always easy and nothing is as easy as succumbing to madness. They might have, in another time, in another place, have called it a broken heart?

An artist could say something like

"I have already said everything that I wanted to say by the age of seventeen"

Well what then?

Tall party. Number something or other. Rudderless, like a paper boat.

"When the gulls take to the city, where are the pigeons meant to go?"

As if that makes sense either.

I get disorientated just saying the word. Disoriented...disorientated, neither looks right in the end.

In the end, neither looks right at all.

*

She wasn't Spanish. She was French.

He said 'Gracias' this time.

She'd brought him his coffee and she thought she'd heard something. She turned.

"Oh...eres de Espana?"

"Er...no. I thought you did."

She looks uncertain.   After scrutinising him she concludes 'You are not Spanish."

"No. I thought you were."

She goes back to her work. When she brings over his orange he asks her if she likes the song.

"Of course.", she shrugs.

"Do you understand what it means?"

She stands back a little.

"Is too early for question.", she frowns. She does pause to listen though. It takes her a few seconds to tune in, her lips move slightly as she hears again the words. "Is New York.", she says with a flourish. "He has nothing. He rides... In New York he has nothing. But so what?"

"You're French?"

She laughs.

"Why not?"

*

She hands me her tobacco.

"Can't I share yours? Your cigarette?"

I get the same look as when I asked her about the song.

"No.", she says. "Please. Help yourself or if you don't want you don't want."

I take the pouch from her.

"You are being very strange."

My phone goes. I have a quick look but it's not important so I ignore it.

"Everyone is strange.", I hear myself saying.

"Why?"

"I don't know. Because they're strange."

She shakes her head and looks away. Or she looks away and shakes her head. There's a bit of a silence that I

112

decide I should break into.

"But is it like this in France?"

"Like what?"

"Do you have all of these things that we have?"

"I don't understand. What things?"

"Shops. Roads. Lamp-posts. Cars. Cafes. Orange juice. Cigarettes."

"No.", she huffs back at me, but with the first hint of a proper smile. "We don't have any of these things. In France there is nothing like this. Only Liverpool you have these things."

"I thought so."

"Of course."

She takes a sharp drag and tilts her head back and blows the smoke up above her.

"It would be a right mess otherwise."

"You are right. Everywhere...there is nothing."

"There'd have to be like millions and millions of lamp-posts if everywhere had them."

"Yes. That would be crazy. Impossible."

She stops and looks thoughtful, a little more serious and questioning.

"Ah. Ah. You mean... You are being… Okay."

"I don't know what I mean. I'm just talking."

"Of course."

"Do you have a pen and paper I can use? Not, like, now, like, when you've finished your smoke. Just while you're not busy."

"If you want?"

"Ta. Gracias. Merci."

"Ok. I will bring."

"Not yet though."

*

"It's about these people. I don't know why. But I have to do something or it will drive me crackers. It sort of fascinates me a bit. There's no way it can be coincidental. What I mean is, one goes up on his own house and just sits there. Or on the flats. Another one is running away from the police, is running across a playing field and climbs up on the clubhouse. Another one sits there with a plastic bag and has, I don't know, his packets of Monster Munch in there or something. There's the odd one that goes up and does some sort of protest with something written on a bedsheet but I don't really count them. I don't like those ones. They're different to these. I only look for the ones who seem to have no real reason and just sit there or stand there. I don't really like it if he starts flinging slates about either but some of them do whether I want them to or not. It's all men. Did I say that? Every one of them. White men. They have to close roads. One was on top of St Helens Town Hall. People coming out from a wedding inside. Police and fire engines everywhere. But none of them jump, see? You think they're up there planning to, you know... But none of them have done anything like that. Not so far anyway. Some of them aren't even all that high enough to, you know... I'm not sure that's what they're about, if that's what they want. I don't know. I just... Nobody seems to be noticing. That's all. No-one is putting them together."

She shakes her head. The other waitress shakes hers too. The fella at the next table pipes up.

"Someone would have noticed. If it's really happening, I mean."

*

"...and that's written when? Six months ago? Seven?
Since then, six more. Seven more. One a month.
Regular. Approximately – I'm saying this, I know it
sounds mad, but it's because I've been noticing – four
or five weeks apart. Not always exactly but on average
not far off. There's usually that gap. One a month. But
no more articles that I've seen, no-one trying to explain
it. Only after the first few and then nothing."

"Because either they don't know what to say or they
don't want to encourage others?"

"Or both. This is what I'm saying. But still."

The Natalies look to each other and shrug. It isn't their
problem and there are customers trying to gain their
attention.

"So what do you reckon?", asks the lad, like I knew he
would.

"I don't know. I can't work out what it means."

"It's like the song then isn't it? You know…"

I am onto that straight away.

"I've thought of the song. People have said that. It'd be

116

nice, but…"

"Yeah. That's it – the tune. 'When this whole world is…' That's it. That's well it."

"No though."

I'm too dismissive too quickly and I don't blame him for looking irritated.

"It makes sense to me.", he says and shifts his weight as he swills around the last of his coffee.

"It doesn't though. Honest. Cos when you look at it - that song was written about, what, Harlem? Brooklyn? Somewhere like that? Those houses and apartment blocks, they had the flat rooftops. They were like legitimate sit-offs. He's not singing about barely being able to balance on a load of dirty old slates and the fire engine coming and the whole street out shouting and buzzing off you. He sings about chilling out, bang out of the way. It's a sit-off. Where the air is clear and free and all that gear."

"Maybe that's it? They go up there and it's, you know, the breeze, and that? Peace and quiet, and that?"

"How long til they hear sirens though or see flashing blue lights? How much peace and quiet would you expect to get? Five minutes, tops, and then you'd realise your whole world is caving in."

"So they haven't thought it through. If they've cracked up..."

"Maybe I'm seeing something that isn't there. And I don't see these lads as being all that much into The Drifters either if I'm honest. I mean, if it was Deacon Blue, still no."

"It does seem..."

"It just wasn't happening before. That's all. And why isn't one person a week in London going up? Or in Birmingham? You can look for yourself on the googling. In America it happens but when it does it's because someone is in a shoot-out or a stand-off or something. There's a reason you can get your head round. Look and you'll see. I've looked. I'm not obsessed with it – well no more than... - but you have a look. There's the odd one here and there. You search again with 'Liverpool' or 'Merseyside' and you can take your pick. And as for there, that article, where it says copycats or Contagion Theory... Bullshit. What do they get out of it? Some of them are just trapped but stay there. Why would anyone copy that? And no matter what kind of trouble you were in before, you've loads more to deal with now. It looks shit. All the street are out talking about you like you're a nuisance. Who'd copy that? Nobody copies something that is absolutely certain to make them look like a massive twat. This is scallies we are talking about. Scousers. Ultra scousers. You only have to look at them."

I show him the images on my phone.

"Scouzers.", I say, to help him out.

He nods.

"Making a show of themselves."

He scrolls through and stares at them.

"Weird.", he says. "They look amazing though. But fucked, like. What are you calling it?"

"I don't know. 'Hey lad, I can't help thinking you've got maybe the wrong lid for that there jigsaw puzzle'. I don't know. Something like that. I'm not very good at titles."

"Maybe they're waiting for one of them tsunamis?"

*

Natalie G takes my plate away. Natalie D is going outside for a smoke and looks to see who will join her. She's quizzed a little about her intentions here and says she came with a plan to set up her own translation business, technical stuff her specialty, things for the university probably, but as she explains all this she admits she is resigned to not bothering with any of it after all. She hands me the cigarette she was about to light for herself.

It's an hour or two later when we are heading up the hill to meet up with some others that one of them asks me "what else?".

I hold open the door as we all file in, trying to think. It takes til we are all settled down in the beer garden for the question to come again.

"It's to do with piracy and slavery. And this city. It wasn't just slavery. It was the piracy as well. We had the best pirates going. You can look them up. Look to someone called Fortunatus Wright, a pearler from over the water. The kiddie. They were chasing him all round the Med. They built ships and recruited crews especially to go after him and catch him. But there was never anything down for them. We had the best techniques. We were boss at privateering. All as we'd do, even though we didn't have the firepower or the big ships that they had, us, we'd go out in smaller ships and catch their attention, they'd be sailing home to France or Italy or Spain weighed down with gold, cotton, cocoa, rum, sugar...I don't know...booty from Napoleonic Wars...stuff they'd robbed or pillaged themselves I suppose. I need to do all the research, but... Yeah. That's the gist of it. We'd go out in skippy little boats and spy out a big heavily laden ship. They'd have all these cannons at the ready and we'd be out in front of them. They'd think it would be sorted in short order, a bit of a laugh even, and set themselves up to blow us out of the water but that's when we'd spin right around, scoot in behind them with the sharper turning circle as they're lumbering about to keep us in their sights, but too slow, too big, too fat and too slow and...this is the thing. You know what we'd do next? You know how we'd knock them right out the game? Finito'ed with just one single shot?"

"Shoot the captain?"

"You might not see him. This worked every time."

"Shoot down the sails?"

"Not with one shot you don't."

"Well go on!"

"Go on!!!"

"We'd shoot off the rudder. One shot and done. It's just a lump of wood, flapping around at the back. And that's that. No rudder, you've got no control. You spin your wheel all you want. You're at our mercy. The battle is won. It's surrendering time. It's not just hand over your gold. It's hands up full stop, if you ever want to see land again. There's not a thing you can do.

Game over."

"That's so cruel."

"Depends how you look at it."

"It's cheating."

"That was just how it goes."

*

"Yous, you should write a song about him. You should. Someone should make a film. He makes our lives – I'm not messing – all of us – he makes us look like nobodies, we're a load of old shabite. And it's not just him. What about this one? Right. Hold on to your hats. This is the one. This Rushton. Edward Rushton. You've never even heard of him. I hadn't. Nobody has. There's statues all over this city, to this fella and that, but there's nothing, there's not even a road named after and virtually all of our streets are named for someone. Listen to this though. He goes off to sea at the age of ten. The ship's boy or something. Ship's lad. Whatever they call it. The look-out in the crows-nest. That sort of thing. You can imagine. He's ten years of age and he's gone to sea. Crazy. Ten. They stop somewhere down in West Africa, some trading post, trading whatever they traded. I've got the books there to find out all the doodah. But regardless, he's there. Maybe he even gets off and goes for a gander around the jungle. Happy days. I don't know. You'd think so. But then they fill up the hold of the ship with cargo and of course the cargo is slaves. Captured slaves. And no matter what you say they can't have been chuffdied about it. It must have been somewhat obvious. Even to this kid. They're not happy are they, the slaves? I mean, we're not happy now. This is the Middle Passage. They might not know exactly what's going on but it's not looking clever. Some of them...rather than be taken aboard... Anyway. Off we go. The kid, he now sees things as they really are. But he's just a kid. What does he know? So it's so far so good and then bad. And then it gets worse. Obviously, for the film, the next thing is the ship hits the rocks, it's bound to happen. It's wrecked and breaks apart and they're all floating about on the edges of the ocean. Right you are. One of the slaves sees the kid bobbing about and pushes a barrel towards him. He grabs it, just as the African lad slips below the waves. He's saved the kid's life. We're all destroyed. Not a dry eye in the house. Or it might have been a woman. I'll check that. It could be important. Ok. Big clichéd Hollywood kick off. Everyone claps and cheers. So what now? What's the next scene after that? Well hang on. He's on another ship and this time he's a couple of years older, maybe twelve, fourteen, thirteen, and again there's a storm and all sorts of hazardous

123

conditions and rocks, big mad rocks there'll have been, and whoever should be in charge of the ship isn't, so he takes over the wheel and steers them though to safety. He's the hero, big time, this time. He has saved the day with all hands accounted for and he's only just getting hairs on his mickey, if you know what I mean. But that's not all of it. On we go, to the third one where the word goes round on board that the slaves have contracted some sort of illness, going right through them, a disease in their eyes, they're all going blind. Somehow he works out a way to treat it. He cleans the infected area and saves their sight, incredible, he's still only a youth, but wouldn't you know it he catches the disease himself. He loses his sight while saving theirs. What a life! What larks! Nobody else knows what to do about it, he runs out of time. So there you are, you're thinking god love him, credits roll. But oh no! He can't see for toffee. But that's not the end of it. He comes home, back to Liverpool. He's no use as a sailor anymore and anyway, besides, he has come to think very seriously about these things, seeing how he has seen what he has seen. He isn't a natural slave trader, put it that way. After what he has experienced he has what you'd call a zealous hatred of the whole business. And he's not particularly quiet about it either. But it's not just that, not just corny tales of having his life saved and the blindness thing. He just...he has just genuinely seen through it. He's not having it. Any of it. You know when you just can't have something anymore? When

124

an idea is just finished? Destroyed? That's what it was, exactly like that. He was determined to bring it down. To shame it out of us. And not for any personal gain or glory. To just smash it up. To just completely obliterate any attempt at justification for it. He was violently opposed. He made the Abolitionists of the day look half-arsed, self-interested. Called anyone who argued with him an apologist. No compromise whatsoever. He wanted to tear the ships apart as they were still being built. He was a pain in the backside to all concerned."

"Ok?"

"He borrowed the money from his sister to take on an alehouse but he kept getting in bother with the press gangs cos he'd hide anyone they were chasing. He was known for it. He opened a bookshop that became like some sort of refuge. He had kids read the news of the day to him. He'd dictate long political poems and even more than that, letters to parliament and letters to the President of the United States of America. He wasn't shy this lad. He wrote to George Washington, kicking off. 'You and all your smart words and you've got a load of slaves', sort of thing. 'I'm onto you'. He was a nuisance. Thomas Paine mentioned something about how advantageous it would be if a bolt of lightning struck Liverpool to silence the republic's most pernicious critic. And he wrote the fucking Rights of Man, unless I'm getting him mixed up with someone else. He was talking about our man Rushton! And

125

what's more, he attracted other like-mindeds and their hangers-on. He had artists and writers of the day come to his yard. It was the busiest port going, don't forget, and from the old world to the new everyone passed through so you'd imagine all sorts came knocking on his door. One of them was a fella called Robert Southey. He was a poet, he mooched around with Coleridge and Byron and those lads. He wasn't as good by the sound of it. You probably haven't heard of him either. Not that I'm any judge but that's what's said. One of my Ma's old books had something: he was made Poet Laureate but that just meant he got stick off all his box of toys for being a bit of a Royalist lackey, he had to write poems in celebration of the glories of the British Army, like a massive sell-out. He must have been like the Gary Barlow or the Elton John of his day. But there he was on the scene all the same. And it's his story, something he wrote, out of all of them, what he did everyone knows today. All the stuff written by the blind bookseller and the others, that's all mostly gone by the thingy. Even the famous ones...none of us could recite a Byron poem. Maybe you can but I can't. It's all hidden away or sometimes it's hard to decipher. His one was easy to remember. But there was some powerful stuff, attacking presidents and governments and long celebratory pieces in praise of the Haitian slave rebellion, Toussaint and that, you'll know, and pleas to the French revolutionaries not to fall into and commit the same errors as their oppressors, there were Irish rebel tales as well. All that, all that sort of thing. But this Southey. He wrote something that everybody knows. Everyone. Everyone learns his story. They can't help but know it. In fact, it might even be the first one anyone ever hears. In English anyway. I don't know about anywhere else."

"Ok."

"Good. So…"

"So what is it?", asks an Irish girl. "Do we know it?"

"What was the first story you learnt, do you think?"

"It'll be something to do with Jesus."

"Before that."

"Before Jesus? Dinosaurs? I don't know."

"I hardly want to tell you now."

"Don't be daft. Get on with it."

"Well it was only simple. I looked him up when I was reading about the blind fella and it said that he wasn't all that accomplished as a poet and there was only the one example of his work worth reading. To be honest it wasn't all that from what I could tell and the book said the same. Something to do with three cheers for the Navy for giving Napoleon the bum's rush. Jingoistic stuff. Not worth anything really. Other poets have got fifty pages and he only gets a page, half a page, not even that, it's shared with someone else."

"So what was it?"

"Come on. Spit it out."

"Come on! Let's go to other place."

"Ok. Ok. Hang on. Ok. Right. It says that he isn't known for anything that has been worth preserving apart from one story believed to be either a traditional tale handed down or else it was assumed to have, you know, come out of nowhere. Anonymous. But it isn't. He wrote it. It didn't write itself. It was him."

"And it was..?"

"The three bears. That was him. Robert Southey. He wrote it."

"You're ridiculous, man."

"Let's be away."

"For Heaven's sake. That isn't even remotely true."

*

"What's this all to do with anything?"

"I don't know. Just something to talk about. But that's what gets me. Down there on Paradise Street and all this going on. Everyone knows about Goldilocks. And you're musicians. You are, you are and…if yous aren't you like you should be. Imagine writing a song that virtually everyone knows and everyone sings but nobody has a clue it was you that wrote it. Wouldn't that be weird? It might take two hundred years but it's heard in every home, maybe it's even the first song a child ever hears and you're the fella or woman who wrote it. How would that be? And it is a proper story when you think about, proper art, because if you really look at it, Goldilocks and the Three Bears…what is it about? What does it mean? What's the moral of the story? It's confusing. It's subtly something…I don't know what though. What's the moral?"

"Well she's…"

"Go on?"

"You… well she eats the porridge"

"And she sits on the chair."

"But what's the moral? What does it teach us?"

"You shouldn't…"

"She sleeps in the bed…"

"Whatever you are going to say, bear this in mind because people forget: she gets off, scot-free, no comebacks. She leaves. She eats the porridge, the one that's spot on. She breaks a chair by sitting on it. Alright, that's an accident. She sleeps in the bed that's just right. But then she fucks off. Never to be seen or heard of again."

"Something happens."

"Don't they eat her?"

"Something…"

"Not from what I've heard. All I remember is that the bears come home and they feel violated. The end. There's no bizzies. She isn't dragged in to court to explain herself, for psychological reports and a social services review and whatnot. She doesn't get a restrictive, what do you call it, one of them things saying you can't go within two hundred yards. She's offski, maybe screwing next door, unplugging their video. Where's the moral behind that? A restraining order, that's it."

"You are asking us here: what is the moral to Goldilocks and the Three Bears?"

"I am. Right now. At ten to ten in the evening. That's your task. You've got til closing time to come up with an answer."

"We're playing another set in a minute. You will have to ask someone else."

"You've got a problem, pal."

"He really has."

"I'm a little bit pissed, I admit it, and stoned, I'm pretty stoned, but apart from that I'm alright. I'm better than I was. I've had a belter day."

"What do you think it is?"

"What is?"

"The moral?"

"I don't know. Fuck the bears? Fuck the bears for even thinking..?   I don't know.   I've thought about it and thought about it some more and I haven't got a clue."

"Why does it have to have a moral?"

"Why tell it to kids otherwise?"

"There doesn't have to always be a moral."

"Everything has a moral. Every day has a moral."

"You are imagining too many things.", says the other one of the Natalies. My favourite one.

*

"The thing is, Maureen, all I'm saying, listen, no listen, don't cry love, listen, it's not what you thing, think, think, it's not what you're thinking, it isn't your fault, it isn't as simple as all that, it might not even all be all my fault, all it is, all I said is, we can't go on living like this, not forever and ever and ever and ever, we just can't, we just, you know, can't, can we? Do you think we can? It's like, it's funny for a bit when you say it, when I say it, it's funny for a while. 'It's not us who's mad it's everyone else'. Sound. Sound as a pound. Stick a fucking sign up. Sorry. No. But here we are. And it's not all that funny anymore. No-one is laughing. I'm not laughing. You're not laughing. Not like we used to. It's just not as funny anymore. Not as much as it used to be, not *funny* funny anyway. It isn't... There's days when... I just don't want to think about it so much. Never mind laugh at it. I can't bear... You just feel so angry. Not you, me. I don't want to go downstairs some days. I do and I don't. Nor do you. I can see it. And I don't even know if it's our fault. If it was just me or just you, but we're both... You know what I mean, don't you? I mean, it's not just this, or us, it's... Do you know where I'm coming from? Do you know what I am trying to say? I don't even know what I'm saying. I just... This is... Just, it's..."

132

*

"But they're all my photos. I don't see what else... I took them all. They're all my pictures."

"That's as maybe."

Lisa sighed heavily, inevitably, like she'd been expecting she'd have to. The moment she heard him say that she gave into it. She knew as soon as he opened his mouth that she was dealing with one of those 'brick-wall-meets-head-banging' situations. It's one of those things people say, "that's as maybe", when they know they're going to remain utterly unhelpful.

For his part, he could see straight away that there was at least a little bit of disdain as well as disappointment in her reaction.

"It is a shame.", was the best he had to offer. "They're very interesting to look at. I just can't give it what it perhaps completely deserves."

She didn't want to say anything. Nothing more needed to be said. Too upset, another word might choke her. She gathered up her bag without looking up at him.

He felt a flush of irritation. She was making this personal.

133

"Don't you want these back?"

He picked up what would have been the centrepiece of the submission – a print of a young man stood on a chimney at dusk with the Anglican Cathedral silhouetted behind his shoulder, a clear primary blue-black drama that reminded him of something he had seen in Matisse. Just that one picture had taken hold of him like nothing he could think of for a decade, for two decades. He didn't know why: he surely didn't want to be the man in the picture, he naturally baulked at even empathetically entering into his world. It looked rotten. He thought he should be able to understand something more deeply about it though. Whatever it was, it was so near. But he couldn't get in. The piece refused him. All he had was a view and that is what gripped his attention. Something has clearly got out of hand. But what? No animal could know such fear as there has to be within that image. No devil either.

Messiah. She'd called it Messiah. After some book, some novel, like she'd have read something that counted for anything that he hadn't even heard of? No, that isn't happening. He felt his frustration to be doubly justified by the cheek of it. But it was certainly true that he was usually much better at this. His criticism was generally well appreciated. He was naturally more attentive to his female students. That's just the kind of fella he was. They sometimes needed a bit of extra guidance. He had spent his entire career welcoming new sensations and encouraged the brighter ones to do the same where appropriate. He could absorb and appreciate the vulnerabilities of others like nobody's business. He'd long ago discarded any commercial thinking and had dedicated himself to artistic distractive entertainment. He'd made up the phrase himself. He'd been supremely pleased with it.

"They're too involved, you see.", he declared. "And you can see their faces. They're all..."

She wasn't listening. She left the door open behind her and managed to hold back the first tears until she was down the first flight of stairs. She knew all of it already. Everything he was about to say she already knew. Of course she knew. She knew that she was dealing with pictures of real people with real problems. Proper living actual people. She knew that in the wrong light it could appear to be exploitative. She knew all of that.

Too close. Too fucked up.

She knew. Of course she did. She wasn't stupid. She's studying art, for fuck's sake. Properly. Properly seriously. But she is worried that nobody seems to be looking. What if nobody wants to know? And why don't they want to look? This might be something. This might be what is happening now. This might be something to do with something. What's the point in any of it if nobody wants to look at what's strange and new? But his "that's as maybe", that was what did for her. Nothing was going to change because of a few of her shitty stupid intrusive photographs.

*

"Could I just take a little look at your pass if that's alright?"

"Oh yes of course. It's in my… Hold on, I did have it. Too many… Sorry."

"Maybe if I check your name?"

"Yes, yes. You can see that I'm… Oh here it is! I knew it was…"

"Oh that's lovely. Thankyou."

"I am on as er…"

"Just checking now."

"I am a bit late, you see. I had a problem with the…"

"There you are. That's lovely."

"…and I'm due to speak at…"

"Two o'clock."

"That's right. Two o'clock."

"Still plenty of time."

"Yes. I hope so. I could do with a coffee. Horrendous trains, you see. I could do with a large glass of wine if I'm honest with you. It's my first time doing, speaking, you know, at this sort of…"

"How exciting!"

"Yes!"

"Lovely."

"Yes. It's the first time that anyone…about this particular…and that's why I'm…"

"Well the best of luck with it."

"Thankyou. Thankyou very much. It's these chaps, you see. They've been… It's to do with…"

"Could you just..? This gentleman I think would like to…this way, sir…could I take a…that's lovely. Thankyou."

"I'll just…I can see that you're…"

"There is a refreshment area for guest speakers. Just ask one of my colleagues. They'll be pleased to help and show you where everything is."

"Oh thankyou. Thankyou."

"That's alright, love. You go and steady your nerves."

"This way is it?"

"No the other way."

"Oh yes. Thankyou. Thanks again."

*

He holds out the license. He lets the man in the oil-stained overalls take it from him to inspect it. All the while he can't take his eyes off the little old freshly sprayed shiny blue motorboat moored at their side: royal blue with a bright white dazzling steering wheel, two bucket seats at the front with what looks like half of a salvaged park bench fitted in behind. No matter. Its rough and readiness added to its charm. He wouldn't want a brand new one. Not for here. It'd have no class.

He doesn't wait for the man to finish reading the paper down to the signatures. He takes an envelope out of his inside pocket and opens it just enough for the man to see the cash. Job done. Hands shaken.

This would be, he is thinking, the happiest purchase he

has ever made in pretty much his entire life. Just at this moment it feels like the only thing he has ever gone out and bought. It's like everything else was leading to this moment. He could, now – he could hardly stop himself from imagining the scenes – he could now drive, pilot, steer, sail...whatever he'd grow to call it, there was nothing on this blue and green earth to stop him going out on most of the lesser canals but even more than that he could take it virtually wherever he wanted to out on the lagoon, going in turn to explore each of the islands. It might take a year to whizz round them all at the speed that this goes. He hasn't even counted them yet on the map. And more, he keeps reminding himself, more than this, whenever anyone comes over to visit he can parade them around to St Mark's Square – get it right, *Piazza San Marco* - as if he owns the place. He still has to learn all the history and the stuff beyond the obvious but he has read enough already and been on a couple of tourist walks.   He could keep them entertained for an hour two just on the *Il Doge* lads. Everything fascinates here. It's hardly been however long but he was already starting to think differently. If what she said was right, and not just her messing about, he might already have begun to walk a little bit like them and thrown about the odd gesture. She'd caught him trying out the accent. He didn't care and it took her ages to stop laughing. He told her to expect that she'll have to get used to it. He was enjoying observing and imitating the manners and mannerisms. It suited him.

139

She asked him how long he thought it all might last – and he didn't know if she was talking about the city or what.   Either way he answered her honestly and sincerely when he told her that all they could see would surely endure forever, if it was up to anyone.

Wait til she sees me turn up in a boat, our own boat, in this, he is thinking.   She won't believe what she sees. He can hardly believe it himself.   The sun is shining so brightly.   You would hardly believe how brightly it shone.   He slowly and carefully plots his way back to find her, canal by canal, corner by corner.

He loves the colours here most out of everything: the morning sun coming out of a mist, perfectly caught and cast to work brushing deepening reds, soaring yellows and youthful sky-blues over houses and rooftops.

He loves the sounds too: the purring chug of the motor and the swirling swishing sploshing of the waters, like inky blackened blood and milk, and the snaking iridescence of the language.

He just completely loves everything.

And then he sees her.   She is standing on the balcony. She looks, she looks unsure.

The poor girl, he thinks.   She must have woken up on her own, she must have been wondering where I went. And she still hasn't seen me.   Not so far.

The End